LADY TEMPTS A ROGUE

Daughters of Desire (Scandalous Ladies)
Book Seven
A Sweet Regency Romance

COLLETTE CAMERON

Blue Rose Romance®

Sweet-to-Spicy Timeless Romance®

LADY TEMPTS A ROGUE
Daughters of Desire (Scandalous Ladies)
A Sweet Inspirational Regency Romance
Copyright © 2023 Collette Cameron®
Cover Art: Jaycee DeLorenzo—Sweet' N Spicy Designs

All Rights Reserved

Attn: Permissions Coordinator
Blue Rose Romance®
PO Box 167
Scappoose, OR 97056
collettecameron.com

eBook ISBN: 978-1955259330
Print Book ISBN: 978-1955259347

Other Collette Cameron Books

Daughters of Desire (Scandalous Ladies)
A Lady, A Kiss, A Christmas Wish
No Lady for the Lord
Love Lessons for a Lady
His One and Only Lady
Never a Proper Lady
Earl of Renshaw
Lady Tempts a Rogue

Check out Collette's Other Series
Castle Brides
Chronicles of the Westbrook Brides
Highland Heather Romancing a Scot
Seductive Scoundrels
The Culpepper Misses
The Honorable Rogues®
Heart of a Scot

Collections
Daughters of Desire Books 1-2
Heart of a Scot Books 1-3
Highland Heather Romancing a Scot Books 1-2
The Honorable Rogues® Books 1-3
The Honorable Rogues® Books 4-6
Seductive Scoundrels Series Books 1-3
Seductive Scoundrels Series Books 4-6
The Culpepper Misses Series 1-2

Dedication

For everyone
who cherishes home and hearth,
but, like me,
also have a wee bit of wanderlust
flowing through their veins.

1

Life is an unpredictable, mysterious journey, is it not?

After having spent several years traveling with Mrs. Westcott, I vowed I would remain in England thereafter. Convinced that I had seen and experienced all that any soul could desire, I was committed to putting down roots and settling into a comfortable, predictable life.

And yet, within a few short months in my most recent position as a companion to an elderly dame who was content to stay home except for attending church, I became so restless, bored, and malcontented that I leaped—yes, very nearly leaped about, clapping my hands, and giggling as if I was queer in the attic—when the opportunity presented itself to travel once again.

Tomorrow night, I set sail for the Mediterranean as a companion to Mrs. Eustacia Peagilly. I do not know when I shall return to England, but I promise to write as I have always done. Do remember me in your prayers, for Mrs. Peagilly, despite her advanced years, is a bold adventurer at heart, and I expect many exciting challenges in the months ahead.

~Miss Trinity Ablethorne, in a letter to hergirlhood friend, Mrs. Purity Mayfield-Rutland

19 October 1818
Daunting Duchess's foredeck
Ten minutes past nine P.M.

*H*ere *I go again, off to who knows where and for God only knows how long.*

The tiniest pang of regret tightened Trinity's throat and cinched her heart before she squared her shoulders, lifted her chin, and pressed her lips into a firm line. *No regrets.* This life of adventure, possible peril, and assured excitement was far better than the mundane, safe, and secure—*boring as Hades*—existence of the past few months.

Perhaps she would have been contented if she were married and had a family...

No. Stop.

Stomping a foot, she gave one sharp shake of her head to dispel *that* wayward thought. At nearly six and twenty, the quixotic but impractical girlhood dream of a husband, four children (two boys and two girls), and a cozy cottage at the shore had been shoved far back on a cupboard shelf. The door had been firmly shut and the key turned in the lock, then tucked away so that temptation would not lure her into peeking inside from time to time to see what might have been.

This was her life, and she had a straightforward choice: to accept her fate or bemoan it.

Practical, resilient, and intrepid, Trinity chose the former.

Come, she chided herself, always one to face self-pity and discouragement with logic and stoicism.

You have much for which to be grateful.

How many women of humble origins have traveled as extensively as you?

Have eaten the rich, tantalizing foods of many cultures?

Have laughed (and also gasped) half in awe and half in astonishment at foreign entertainment and unique customs?

A gull landed on a nearby piling. Head cocked, the gray and white creature observed the tumult aboard the ship and then turned its tiny, black button eyes on her. The wind ruffled the bird's tail feathers, and it flapped its wings twice.

"Shouldn't you be tucked snuggly in your nest?" she asked the inquisitive bird. "Or wherever birds of your kind sleep?"

The gull flapped its wings again and took flight, circling above her once before gliding toward the chimney stacks a few streets away.

Pulling the hood of her serviceable woolen cloak farther over her head to prevent the breeze nipping at her cheeks from making her ears ache, Trinity scanned her gaze over the scruffy crew bustling about the deck with practiced skill before shifting her regard to the much less active East India Docks below.

This time of night, the wharf was vacant except for a trio of loudly singing, obviously pished sailors, a pair of scantily attired ladies of the evening—both revealing a shocking display of bare legs and voluptuous bosoms—and a tired appearing fellow, knitted hat pulled low over his forehead as he hunched into his jacket and lumbered down the long expanse.

From somewhere nearby, bawdy laughter, the lively strains of a fiddle, and more slurred singing carried seaward on the tangy river breeze.

Cleaner and less malodorous than several of the other docks Trinity had visited over the years, the East India Docks' pungent odors would, nevertheless, put off a less stalwart female.

Many a *beau monde* dandy too, she would wager.

The recipient of raw sewage and other equally noxious substances, the River Thames reeked to high heaven. Not enough to compel Trinity to cover her nose with her crochet-edged and lemon-water-scented handkerchief tucked into her inside cloak pocket but enough to prevent her from totally filling her lungs with the fetid air.

Realizing that she held each breath a second or two, Trinity released her current partial lungful in a small whoosh that created a miniature vapor cloud. Making a rueful face, she chuckled at her silliness. Sailing in

October wasn't ideal, but she'd spend the winter in warmer climes, and that was much preferable to England's drizzly, bone-penetrating dampness.

At the docks' far end, a rickety hackney drawn by a sway-backed horse trundled along the cobbles, its wheels echoing hollowly in the gray, fog-shrouded atmosphere. A black cat darted in front of the coach, its tail pointed straight as it fled an invisible foe.

Not superstitious or given to frightening easily, Trinity nevertheless could not stave off the shudder scuttling from her waist to her nape and then padding across her shoulders like a kitten tiptoeing on a prickly bush.

A premonition?

Of what?

A deckhand yelling an ear-burning curse dragged her attention back to the commotion around her.

A wry grin pulled her mouth upward at the sides.

These past years, she had acquired knowledge of vulgar vocabulary that would cause Mrs. Hester Shepherd, the proprietress of the foundling home and school where Trinity had spent her childhood, to blush crimson.

Having been raised to be a proper lady, Trinity had never let such uncouth expletives pass her lips. But should she ever require a hardy curse guaranteed to make one's ears burn, she could summon several creative and physically impossible expletives with no effort whatsoever.

That she did not understand what half of them meant was of no consequence.

The *Daunting Duchess*—such a regal name for a rather nondescript frigate—sailed in less than an hour at high water.

Trinity's attention drifted toward the dock.

Odd that the captain had not ordered the gangway removed yet.

Weren't all the passengers aboard?

A tendril of hair that had escaped her neat chignon tickled her cheek.

Frowning, she brushed it aside.

Late this afternoon, when she and Mrs. Peagilly—presently enjoying a cup of ginger tea to stave off seasickness—boarded the vessel, Captain Horatio Breckett mentioned that seven other passengers also sailed to Morocco.

Trinity's girlhood friend, Faith Kellinggrave, and her new husband, Lord Constantine, were to have voyaged on the ship too. Unfortunately, Lord Constantine's father, the Duke of Landrith, had suffered a serious riding accident, causing the postponement of Faith's wedding trip until he recovered.

Besides two businessmen, Amos Truman-Shelton and Lawrence Meriwether, Trinity had met the diplomat, Sir Godfrey McKinnick, his wife, Martha, and their two freckle-faced children, Gladys and Georgie— a thumb-sucking little chap still in short pants.

That left one passenger unaccounted for, though they might've boarded before Trinity and Mrs. Peagilly and, if a poor sailor, tucked themselves into their berth for what might be an unpleasant day or two or three.

Trinity had suffered horrid malaise on her first ocean voyage, but never again, thank God. Such was not the case for everyone, and she was most grateful her body had somehow adjusted to the sea's churning and bobbing so that sickness never afflicted her again. She'd truly thought she would die those first several hours and pitied those suffering seasickness for days on each voyage.

Earlier, when Mrs. Peagilly assured Trinity she could spare her company, her employer had also vowed that as long as she drank ginger tea, she would not succumb to nausea.

Trinity glanced to where the full moon hung in the sky, but given the almost eerily fine mist shrouding the horizon, the distant orb only managed a faint, silvery glow. The captain must be confident the haze would lift or, at the very least, disperse as they headed out to sea.

Trinity certainly hoped so.

She did not want the rolling fog to steal her last view of England's shoreline or obstruct the glittering stars above. The nocturnal lights appeared much more vivid and ever so much closer over the ocean than on land.

She'd always considered celestial navigation an extraordinary skill. Had she been a man, she might've pursued a life at sea. Years ago, she had borrowed a book from Glen Furrows, the sailing master on the *Liberty June,* about navigation using the stars. Scrunching her nose, she tried to recall the thin tome's title, but memory failed her.

Hunched into her wrap, a comfortable Kersey woolen shield against the evening's permeating chill, she staunchly determined not to go below until England's shoreline disappeared—which might be far sooner than she liked given the uncooperative weather, dash it all.

During the first couple of years traveling the Continent and other marvelous locales with her first employer, Mrs. Wescott, Trinity had enjoyed herself immensely. For certain, at the onset, she'd been homesick for England, but orphaned and raised in a foundling home, Trinity had no one waiting for her or anyone who cared about her, other than a few friends from her time at Haven House and Academy for the Enrichment of Young women.

Mrs. Wescott provided Trinity, a girl of unimpressive origins, with an opportunity of a lifetime. While Mrs. Wescott had preferred frequenting traditional and popular tourist sites, Mrs. Peagilly was a whole other precocious and tenacious creature. Far more adventurous and less attached to creature comforts than Mrs. Wescott, Mrs. Peagilly *relished the unexpected and scintillating adventure.*

Those were her own words.

Once, the courageous woman had found a juvenile, four-foot python asleep on her cot.

"I had left the tent unfastened, you see," Mrs. Peagilly recounted. "And the poor thing found a cozy place to curl up and take a snooze away from the elements."

Poor thing?

Trinity doubted her response would've been as sympathetic as Mrs. Peagilly's.

No indeed.

No matter their size, snakes were unpleasant, scaly, clammy, slithery creatures.

Was slithery a word?

The shudder that rippled over her this time was *not* from the cold.

Trinity had despised snakes for as long as she could remember. An encounter with a hissing, three-foot grass snake while playing in the garden when she was five had sent her shrieking into the orphanage. It had been months before she entered the garden or walked in the grass again. To this day, she would not venture into grass taller than her ankles.

And yet, here Trinity was headed to Morocco, home to puff adders, horned vipers, cobras, and boas.

Yes, but that did not mean she needed to venture into the nasty creatures' habitats.

She put a gloved finger to the dimple in her chin. Mayhap she should acquire a pistol, or at the very least, a stout stick—a large, very stout stick.

A mélange of heady expectation and sensible wariness wrestled for dominance as she considered what experiences she might encounter with her new employer.

"We need to move the gangway soon, Cap'n, else we shall miss the tide."

Trinity half-turned toward the speaker, Thaddaeus Compton.

The second mate—a ruggedly handsome chap in his late thirties or early forties—clasped his hands behind him as he rocked back on his heels.

"It'll be tricky enough navigating the river with this

pea soup fog," Mr. Compton said.

Scanning his keen gaze over the pier, Captain Breckett puffed out his pewter gray bewhiskered cheeks, then gave a stern nod.

"Wait five more minutes, Mr. Compton. Not a second more."

"Aye, Cap'n."

The *clip-clop, clip-clop* of a horse approaching captured Trinity's attention. The hackney lurched to a bumpy stop before the *Daunting Duchess*'s pier.

"At last." Relief riddled the captain's two clipped words. "I was not positive he would make it, and sailing without him would've put me in a"—he sent Trinity a covert glance— "deuced smelly kettle of fish."

So they *had* been waiting for a passenger.

A very tardy and mysterious passenger.

Whomever they were, they must be important, indeed, to cause the captain to tarry until the last minute—the last five minutes—that was.

"I do not know why you waited on the bloody blighter." Contempt for the inconsiderate passenger permeated Mr. Compton's tone. He swerved his deep brown-eyed gaze toward Trinity.

"Beg your pardon, Miss Ablethorne."

"'Tis of no consequence, Mr. Compton."

Trinity waved away his apology.

11

He knew as well as she did that she would hear much worse on the voyage. In fact, the captain's *kettle of fish* was no doubt for her benefit—to spare her tender sensibilities. The only way for women to avoid crude speech on a ship was to remain in their cabin with cotton stuffed in their ears, and that she had no intention of doing.

Snapping his timepiece shut with a portentous *click*, Captain Breckett glanced upward at the mainmast, where an agile young man clambered up the stout pole, and then to the foremast, where another sailor in a navy peacoat secured an encased lantern.

"Because, Mr. Compton," the captain said with a side-eyed glance and a subtle jerk of his chin toward the newcomer, "*he* is one of the ship's owners."

"I beg your pardon, sir." Mr. Compton dipped his square chin. "I meant no disrespect."

Trinity was quite certain he had meant exactly that.

The captain merely grunted, and the second officer wended his way to the foredeck.

To better observe the ramshackle vehicle below, Trinity pushed her hood back a few inches. Not wishing to appear a snoop or busybody but unable to contain her curiosity, she lowered her head and peeped through her eyelashes.

One of the owners, hmm?

Wasn't that interesting?

Then why the hired hack?

Something was not quite right.

A tall man jumped out, a bulging satchel in his gloved hand. Covered from head to toe in a dark cape, he sprinted effortlessly up the gangway. The instant he set foot on deck, the men responded to a silent signal from the captain and scrambled to detach the gangplank. A bell tolled, announcing the ship's imminent departure.

The mysterious man, his features hidden in the hood of his black cloak, gave Captain Breckett a terse nod. Though Trinity could not see his eyes, she was certain his attention veered to her for an instant just as the wind whipped off her hood.

He visibly stiffened, causing the captain to send her a speculative glance before the ship's owner disappeared below deck. He had not spoken a word.

Without a doubt, someone had prearranged the owner's arrival.

Why the clandestine nature and secretiveness?

The captain and the first officer, Jack Alderton, a Scot as short and squat as Mr. Compton was tall and lithe, shouted orders. Men scurried hither and yon, and Trinity tapped her forefinger to her mouth as the *Daunting Duchess* slipped from her moorage.

Who was the enigmatic passenger, possessing

power enough to delay the ship's sailing?

There were so many possibilities.

Did he even sail under his real name?

Probably not.

Which begged the question, why?

Well, Trinity had weeks to find out.

She always enjoyed a good puzzle.

As she pulled her hood over her head once more, she recalled his sudden rigidness when he'd seen her.

Did that mean he recognized her?

Now there was an interesting notion because, other than a single house party when she had first returned to England and tea on one occasion at Dr. and Joy Morrisette's, Trinity had not been anywhere other than services at St. George's with Mrs. Templemore.

Somehow, the latter seemed the least likely of the trio.

That left the tea and house party.

No, that left the house party. An intimate affair, the tea had consisted of a few close friends. This furtive fellow had not been amongst them.

Though tempted to follow the mysterious stranger below, Trinity resisted. He was not going anywhere, and she would not deprive herself of this last glimpse of England. Besides, what would she do?

Linger outside his cabin like a demented ninny?

A grin teased the corners of her mouth as she rested her elbows on the ship's rail.

What might've proved a rather unexceptional voyage had become decidedly more intriguing.

2

Your constant manipulation and interference have brought me to this juncture. When you dared to scheme to entrap me into marriage with a bird-witted chit, scarcely out of the schoolroom and possessing less acumen than a trained poodle, you left me no choice.

Thank God, Miss Marsters-Montgomery can neither tell time nor knows her left from her right, else you would be left to explain to Lord Poindexter why I refused to marry his compromised daughter. My ears still ring with the echoes of Lady Hornbellow's shrieks upon Miss Marsters-Montgomery climbing into her bed at three in the morning at the Bickerstaffs' house party.

You should thank God that the girl did not mistakenly crawl into a rogue's bed, for several were in attendance that week. Mark my words: that poor chit will end up heavy with child and with no ring on her finger if her father doesn't take heed and stop these preposterous shenanigans.

~Mr. Devin Everingham, in a terse letter to his mother, Mrs. Desdemona Everingham

Five minutes later
Below deck — passenger cabins

After kicking the small door shut behind him, Devin tossed his satchel on the narrow lower bunk. The thud said much about the state of the hard, thin mattress and the minimal comfort it would offer him each night.

As he unfastened the silk frogs at his throat, he examined the small cabin. Having been delivered earlier in the week, his two travel trunks sat side by side across from the bunks, scarcely leaving enough room to walk between the double berth and the luggage.

Fastened to the wall at the far end of the closet-like cabin stood a washstand with a plain white basin and pitcher nestled in cutouts to secure them. A metal clasp held a single hinged wood panel in place, which passed for a desk and dining table. A scuffed chair occupied the space beneath the makeshift desk.

This humble berth was to be Devin's home for the coming days. Not a luxurious stateroom by half, but adequate for his needs, which sufficed. The voyage to Casablanca took a week, give or take a day or two. He could abide these uncomfortable accommodations without complaint.

The shouts of the crew filtered below as the men readied the ship to leave port. A peculiar feeling swelled behind his ribs, which took him a moment to identify as pride. This vessel was partially his, thanks to his father.

Guilt, raw and sharp, scraped across his conscience.

Truth be told, Devin ought to have put off his carousing and taken on his father's mantle years ago.

17

He could not change the past, but by thunder, he could forge a different future—one that would not fill him with disgust and shame but rather pride and a sense of accomplishment.

Father had always maintained that every soul had a preordained destiny and purpose, yet most of mankind missed the mark for a myriad of reasons. But then again, Father had been a man of faith, even after he'd succumbed to liquor's temptation.

Sighing and shoving aside the melancholy reflections, Devin steered his thoughts to the present.

He had deliberately waited until the last moment to arrive at the ship.

Yes, he was a grown man with a mind of his own, but thwarting a woman as determined and manipulative as his mother was not easy. Her obsession with him marrying into the peerage bordered on unbalanced, and he suspected she would only consider the failure of her latest plan as a temporary setback.

Hence the drastic measures he had taken to foil her.

More than once, she'd spied upon his activities, and that was why, after her most recent debacle, Devin had asked Milton Shillingford, his man of business and trusted friend, to find him lodgings, deliver his letter requesting passage on the *Daunting Duchess*, pack and transport Devin's possessions, and even hire the hack that brought him to the docks this night.

All managed through Shillingford's tangled network of contacts, making it difficult for dear Mama to discover Devin's whereabouts.

He curled one side of his mouth upward in disgust.

A child should not have to outmaneuver their interfering, intrusive parent.

Ill-advisedly…recklessly…or negligently—it did not matter which—Devin had permitted his mother too much leeway for far too long. In truth, he ought to have reigned her in years ago. But consumed with living a rakehell's debauched life and grieving his father's death, he had unintentionally provided her opportunity.

By the time he came to his senses and realized the error of his ways, Mama had become overly confident of her imagined power. He was as much to blame as she. Had he nipped her overreach in the bud, she would not have become the out-of-control monster she now was.

The morning after Miss Marsters-Montgomery had mistaken Lady Hornbellow's bedchamber for his, Devin had faced himself in the looking glass. Such self-loathing had consumed him that he had determined at that moment to set things to right.

No more drunkenness.

No more carousing.

No more deflecting responsibility and duty.

And of topmost import, no more enabling his mother's interference.

Surprising even himself—for he was quite new at this chivalry stuff—he'd written the Dowager Viscountess Poindexter, informed her of her granddaughter's humiliating incident, and implored her to remove Miss Marsters-Montgomery to a safer environment.

Sadly, the dowager had not responded.

Short of spiriting Miss Marsters-Montgomery away, Devin's hands were tied. The law should not permit a father to jeopardize his child's safety or use her as a pawn—particularly a young woman with dubious intelligence.

The ship pitched, a slow, gentle roll, and Devin braced his hand against the wall.

Though a partial owner of the *Daunting Duchess*—a portion of his inheritance from Father—Devin had not sailed before.

Please, God, grant me the stomach for sea travel.

It mattered not if he was not a good sailor.

When he'd sent the message requesting Captain Breckett reserve him a cabin aboard the *Daunting Duchess*, he had been livid and a trifle desperate. He had breathed a sigh of relief and slept through the night for the first time since the incident with Miss Marsters-

Montgomery when Captain Breckett's terse response arrived.

Cabin reserved.
Departure 19 October-evening tide.
Do not be late.
Shall sail without you.
Breckett

Devin had narrowly escaped the plot hatched between his interfering mother and the wily Viscount Poindexter. For years, his mother had attempted to matchmake. But that…*that*…

Hell's chiming bells.

He could not even finish the thought without ire billowing behind his breastbone and several colorful invectives tapping at the back of his teeth.

Mother had gone too far this time.

Far, *far* beyond the pale, and it would be some time before he forgave her—if ever.

A sweet thing, fifteen or sixteen, Miss Marsters-Montgomery was not the brightest candle in the chandelier. In fact, Devin suspected that was one reason her negligent father had consented to the madcap scheme. Shame on the vile rotter for exploiting his daughter and putting her in harm's way.

No saint himself, Devin was not such a blackguard that he would take advantage of the girl. However, there were plenty of scapegraces and libertines that would've done. Mother had counted on him being an honorable gentleman should the girl be compromised.

Good thing it had not come to that because he would not have asked for Miss Marsters-Montgomery's hand. And the girl would've been ruined beyond redemption.

Eyes narrowed, Devin studied a four-inch scrape on the wall and scratched his nose.

Was he more rogue than gentleman or more gentleman than rogue?

That he did not know twisted his gut, and the mass lay there coiled, making him the merest bit woozy.

Or was that the ship's movements?

He snorted and shook his head as he whipped his cloak off, then hung it on a convenient peg beside the door before removing his triple-caped great coat and hanging it on another peg. With a grimace, he plowed a hand through his hair before rotating his neck several times in a vain attempt to loosen the pebbles that had taken up residence in his neck and shoulder muscles.

Knots caused by constant tension.

That he should have to sneak around London for these past weeks, staying in one lodging house after another, under ever increasingly ridiculous false names, to avoid his meddlesome mother's intrigues was beyond galling.

The disconcerting truth was that Mother had shown no remorse after Miss Marsters-Montgomery botched the seduction attempt. Devin doubted his mother would voluntarily eschew her machinations. So, rather than risk entrapment in wedlock, he'd opted to take a personal interest in a few of Father's investment ventures abroad.

Specifically, those farthest from England's shores.

Though Devin was an only child, he intended to stay away for a lengthy while—long enough for Mother to become a jot repentant. He had no plans to inform her when he returned to England either.

Like delicate eggshells, trust, once broken, was not something easily mended.

Perched on the edge of the lower berth, he unlocked the first trunk and, after lifting the lid, took swift inventory. As Devin did not retain a valet—another disappointment to his class-conscious mother—Shillingford had seen his belongings packed.

Mama was so bent on Devin marrying into the peerage, yet she had married a wealthy merchant. And by all that was sacred and holy, never, *never* let poor berated and beleaguered Father forget that he was beneath her. She had driven him to drink with her constant harping and complaining. Any love they may have once shared had dissipated after years of haranguing and criticism.

If that was what love and marriage did to a man, Devin wanted no part of matrimony.

Heaving a sigh, he closed the first trunk, the lid clunking shut with a small *thunk*.

The other trunk stood upright and opened like an armoire but must remain closed except when he required something, or else he could not pass between it and the berth. Falling back onto the thin, hard mattress, he clasped his hands behind his neck and stared at the slats above him.

Zounds.

Imagine if two people shared this inadequate space.

He eyed his large trunks through half-closed eyes.

Those would not be here if he'd had to share, and he made a mental note to thank the captain. The cramped cabin might not be luxurious, but at least Devin had privacy.

The ship's manifest listed him as Silas Fenby, and he had not yet decided whether to continue using the false name throughout the voyage.

There was no point in doing so now.

A pretty oval face framed by sable curls invaded his musings.

He *had* seen her before—the woman on the deck—

but where or when, he could not recall.

Were her eyes blue?

The muted light made it impossible to tell for certain.

Did she recognize him too?

The gentle motion of the ship revealed they'd set sail, and Devin sat upright. He might as well go above and watch as London disappeared from view. An unexpected sense of anticipation and exhilaration gripped him.

He might've taken this course to prove a point and to escape his mother's machinations, but it was time for him to step into his father's shoes. At least to the degree that Father had been an astute businessman—not the unsavory, drowning-his-sorrows-in-spirits part.

Besides, the young woman might still be on deck.

Devin quirked his mouth into a sarcastic grin as he eschewed his great coat and wrapped his cloak about his shoulders again. Here he was fleeing England because of a woman, rather because of *women*, and he was about to go above deck because of a pretty face.

Well, old chap. You aren't dead.

Just reluctant to enter the parson's mousetrap.

He'd heard that voyages could be quite tedious— days on end with nothing to do but read, sketch, play cards...

A shipboard flirtation could not cause any harm.

As long as Devin was mindful to keep it just that—a mild, carefree liaison.

The ship pitched slightly, and his stomach followed suit.

Bloody perfect.

Not even out to sea yet, and his innards quaked like a flag buffeted by a stiff breeze.

A hand braced against the doorframe, he drew in a purgative breath.

Surely the fresh air above would help calm his budding nausea.

In hindsight, two bowls of beef stew and apple cobbler for dinner mightn't have been wise.

Jaw clenched, he retraced his passage of several minutes ago.

He would either improve on deck or disgrace himself.

Would not that give the crew a good laugh?

The *Daunting Duchess*'s owner casting up his accounts in full view of everyone.

3

I promise to consider coming to live with you and your new bride after this excursion, but that doesn't mean I shall do so. You know I treasure my independence. Besides, you and Charlotte need time alone. Marriage is an adjustment, no matter how deeply in love you are.

I may be alone in this world, except for you and Charlotte, but I refuse to become a burdensome old tabby. We shall discuss the possibility when I return to England in a few months.

I might be more inclined to forsake my wandering ways if I had a grandniece or grandnephew to dote upon.

~Mrs. Eustacia Peagilly, in a letter to her nephew,
the Vicar Willard Howard
Posted the day she sailed from London aboard the
Daunting Duchess

Daunting Duchess – main deck

The swirl of fog clinging to Britain's shoreline, like lovers reluctant to separate, cleared as the ship sailed smoothly toward the Atlantic. Trinity's disappointment at not being able to see England fade from view quickly turned to delight as she craned her neck and studied the clear, ebony sky.

Her hood crumpled to settle upon her shoulders, and the breeze had increased to a bone-chilling degree. Her ears would undoubtedly get cold, perhaps resulting in an earache, but she could not regret the sacrifice for the splendid view.

"Cassiopeia and Perseus," she whispered to herself in awe.

October evenings were ideal for spotting the pair of constellations in the northern sky, but this was the first time she had seen either this clearly. An amateur, self-taught astronomer, her fascination with stars extended to constellations too. She had purchased a constellation map in Italy several years ago and brought it with her on all her journeys. Her journal contained several rough sketches as well.

"Look to the right, and you can see Pegasus too."

She glanced over her shoulder.

Mr. Compton stood six feet away, handsome and commanding in his navy-blue uniform.

"Really?" She peered upward, trying to locate the mystical horse.

"Here, use my night telescope." He withdrew the brass instrument behind his back and extended it toward her after opening it to its full length. "It is not the most powerful spyglass, but it will magnify the stars."

How long had he observed her?

Long enough to fetch his telescope.

She was both flattered and disconcerted.

Nonetheless, Trinity could not resist.

"Thank you, Mr. Compton. I believe I shall."

Grinning, she accepted the slender rod.

Yes, proper young ladies were supposed to smile demurely, but really, a grin was so much more appropriate at times like this.

She raised the telescope, and a small gasp escaped her.

"Oh, this is simply magnificent. Marvelous."

Mr. Compton edged closer but kept a respectable distance between them as they looked upward.

"You have an interest in astronomy, Miss Ablethorne?"

Giving an eager nod, she continued peering at the innumerable twinkling jewels. "I certainly do. I am not very adept at identifying many constellations, but I have learned a few. I have also read a book about celestial navigation."

Why was she telling him all of this?

Because she tended to prattle when nervous, and Mr. Compton made her nervous.

Lowering the glass, she cut him a sidelong look as she swept her free hand in an arc. "Doesn't it make you feel small and insignificant, considering the vastness of what God has created?"

"I am not religious, but I take your meaning." He presented his strong profile. "It is rather humbling, is it not? The immensity of the ocean and sky?"

"Mr. Compton, a moment if you please." Captain Breckett bid his second in command attend him on the quarterdeck.

Trinity passed the telescope back. "Thank you again. It is truly quite a spectacular invention."

"My pleasure, Miss Ablethorne. I hope we may study the stars together again many times on the voyage."

Did he indeed?

Did Trinity want to?

She was not certain, but she would like to avail herself of his telescope in the future.

"And perhaps I may take you for a stroll or tea when we reach Casablanca. I know of a local coffee shop serving delicious coffee, tea, and pastries."

That would depend entirely on Mrs. Peagilly.

Trinity angled her head in response.

He flashed her a rather disarming smile before striding away. She was not altogether positive the queer fluttering in her stomach was a good thing.

The persistent wind had loosened several strands of

hair, and they whipped about her face. She shoved them behind her ears and dragged her hood atop her head again. Her skirts and cloak billowed around her ankles, the fabric snapping as it strained in one direction and then another.

"A conquest already, my dear young lady?"

With the crew calling orders back and forth, a couple of the men even singing a jaunty ditty, and the creaks and groans of the vessel underway, Trinity had not heard Mrs. Peagilly's light tread as she approached.

"Hardly." Good heavens, what a notion. "Mr. Compton was simply being helpful."

Wasn't he?

Trinity stepped sideways over a coiled length of rope so Mrs. Peagilly could join her at the ship's rail.

"How was your tea?" she asked, presenting her back to the wind.

"Honestly, I am not overly fond of ginger. It is rather vile stuff. Regardless, it is an effective tonic." Wrinkling her nose, Mrs. Peagilly patted her middle. "A cup thrice a day, and my stomach remains as tranquil as if we sailed across a sea of glass. I do have the beginnings of a headache." She put trembling fingers to her forehead. "I hope it does not turn into a—"

The sound of retching brought her up short.

As one, they turned in the direction of the distraught

31

passenger—the ship owner hanging over the rail, sagging like a wilted daisy.

"Poor fellow. If he is this wretched now in this calm water, wait until we make the open sea." Mrs. Peagilly cocked an eyebrow under her violet bonnet. "And should we encounter a storm…"

Clucking, she shook her head.

"Indeed," Trinity murmured, moved to compassion for the man who had drawn mocking attention from the unsympathetic crew.

Were they aware he was the ship's owner?

If so, they ought to show more respect.

On the other hand, considering the secrecy surrounding his arrival, they might not know. Still, taking delight in another's misfortune revealed a lack of character.

A half smug, half disgusted expression creased Mr. Compton's features before he returned his attention to Captain Breckett and the first officer, Mr. Alderton, once more.

Was Mr. Compton still miffed that the captain had delayed weighing anchor on the owner's behalf?

It was not as if they'd missed the tide.

Only having known the second mate for a matter of hours, Trinity was not sure what kind of man he was. One moment, he was all solicitous courtesy, but the next, he unabashedly directed scorn to someone he ought to show a degree of respect.

Mrs. Peagilly patted Trinity's arm. "I shall go below and have more tea brewed. It may be too late for the gentleman, however."

She cast the distraught fellow a considering glance.

"Trinity, see if you can find someone to assist you in helping him below. The longer he remains up here heaving, the weaker he'll become, and then getting him to his cabin will be a devilish challenge."

"Of course," Trinity murmured, not at all certain she should approach a stranger in distress and even more unsure who to ask for help. Perhaps one of the businessmen she had met earlier.

A swift perusal of the deck revealed neither was up here. Nor were the McKinnicks.

"There's a dear. I knew I liked you. You remind me of me when I was your age. Smart, courageous, but also kind and empathetic."

After another pat on Trinity's forearm, Mrs. Peagilly picked her way across the deck, maneuvering around sailors and equipment with the ease of someone accustomed to moving about on ships.

Trinity had never asked her new employer how many voyages she'd undertaken. She did, however, know that childless and widowed early in life, Mrs.

Peagilly had spent decades traveling the world.

Slightly uncomfortable at approaching the stranger but compelled by sympathy, Trinity made her way toward him, sending more than one smirking sailor a quelling glare.

Why must people be so unkind?

Not everyone was a good sailor.

There was no crime in that.

The wind persisted in teasing the folds of his black cloak, but such was his misery that he seemed not to notice.

"*Ahem.*"

Trinity stood a mere three feet away, but the man, his white-knuckled hands gripping the rail he hunched over, also appeared unaware of her presence.

"Excuse me, sir."

Slowly, as if he feared sudden movement would send the contents of his stomach spewing forth again, he lifted his head and turned ever so slightly in her direction. His grayish-green pallor induced another wave of sympathy.

No one relished an audience when they were ghastly ill.

Gaze unfocused, his eyes so dark they appeared black in the muted light, he blinked, then blinked again.

Trinity could not pull her attention from his face,

though her prolonged stare went beyond inquisitiveness into downright rudeness.

But those eyelashes.

Envy prickled her, and the sensation was most discomfiting.

Really. It was criminal for a man to possess such thick, lush lashes.

Moreover, the rest of his vaguely familiar features were just as striking. At least they appeared so in the shadowy half-light. Aware she had crossed the mark into impoliteness, Trinity, nevertheless, looked her fill.

High cheekbones, shadowed by dark stubble, slanted downward to a strong, angular jaw. The wind played her fingers through his neatly trimmed dark brown wavy hair, the color of freshly poured coffee with just a touch of milk added—a shade lighter than his lashing eyebrows.

A groan escaped him, and he clenched his jaw and shut his eyes for a second.

Trinity well knew how he suffered.

He truly was a pitiful wretch, and the voyage had scarcely begun. Hopefully, he would adjust to the motion swiftly, or misery would be his unending company.

"I beg your pardon, sir, but you appear to need assistance."

He did not so much as bat an eyelash in acknowledgement that Trinity had spoken.

She tried a different tact.

"My employer, Mrs. Peagilly, has gone below to have ginger tea prepared for you. She vows it will settle your stomach. She drinks it herself. Thrice a day. It works wonders for her. She bid me help you to your cabin, else you become…too…weak."

Trinity stuttered to a stop.

As was her wont, she'd been prattling in her nervousness.

Poor man.

The last thing he needed was her chattering like a magpie.

She squared her shoulders and firmed her lips.

"Here, I shall assist you." She sidled closer and slipped an arm around his firm waist. He was taller than she but not as tall or lean as Mr. Compton. Not that he was given to fat by any means.

No, a thick layer of muscles rippled beneath her fingers curled around his ribs.

Having never touched a man in such a familiar way, she could not ascertain if her breathlessness was from discomfit or something a trifle naughtier.

"Awfully forward, aren't you?" The man managed a lopsided grin as he slung an arm around her shoulders.

"We have not been introduced," he managed in a hoarse whisper.

He cared about social proprieties when he vomited in public?

"Well, there is no one to do the job properly," she said with false cheerfulness. "So we will have to skip that convention. I, for one, think there are far too many unnecessary and ridiculous strictures in any event."

"Amen," he muttered.

Amen?

Trinity grunted as he leaned into her, and they shuffled forth—not an easy task with the swaying ship and the man's uneven gait. This man was no weak fop or soft dandy either. No, he was sleek, corded muscle, and her stomach did that strange fluttery thing again.

Only this time, it assuredly was not unpleasant.

She tucked that tidbit into the back of her mind to examine at a more opportune moment.

"I am Trinity Ablethorne, companion to Mrs. Eustacia Peagilly. We are on our way to Morocco."

For pity's sake.

She rolled her eyes heavenward at her stupidity.

They were *all* sailing to Morocco.

Supporting his weight disrupted her breathing, and she panted from exertion as she gauged how far the ladder-like steps to the lower decks were—too dashed far with the fellow drooped upon her like limp pastry on a pie. She had no idea how she would maneuver him down the risers without them taking a tumble.

She gave him a side-eyed glance, surprised to see him staring at her, three creases puzzling his brow.

He narrowed those dark eyes.

"Or perhaps…" He spoke slowly and deliberately, the effort costing him much as he paled further. "Perhaps, I have actually died—I have asked God to let me do so for the past several minutes—and you are an angel sent to guide me to heaven."

Had he been drinking too?

Leaning a fraction nearer, Trinity gave a surreptitious sniff but detected only wind, sea, and a slightly spicy-woodsy cologne but no strong spirits.

His frown deepened, crinkling his eyes to thin slits.

"Though, I was not certain I would end up in heaven and not hell, where I probably belong."

Trinity had been seasick and did not remember being as confused as this man was.

He put an unsteady hand to her hair, once again exposed as her hood had slipped off when she snaked her arm around his sculpted ribs.

"I thought angels had white hair. Yours is sable. Sleek and soft as an American mink."

Mink?

She puzzled her forehead.

What kind of creature was that?

"Mink."

"Yes, my father dabbled in fur trading for a short while. The mink pelts are lovely, soft, and luxurious, but Father could not abide killing animals for their fur. Many thought that made him weak, but it took courage to oppose what he steadfastly believed immoral when most others found the practice acceptable."

"I agree. However, I am no angel but a flesh and blood woman," she said crisply.

It would not do for him to form a wrong idea about her.

"A very soft and nice-smelling woman."

He sniffed her hair. "Mmm, you smell good. Like summer flowers."

Good Lord.

Shaking her head, Trinity made a scoffing sound. "You are too ill to make any sense. Save your breath and strength."

They crossed beneath a lantern just as she glanced upward and caught his face in full light.

Everything snapped into place as memory rushed back to her.

She recognized him then.

Devin Everingham.

"I remember you," she said. "I thought you looked familiar. You were at the Mumfords' house party in August."

It *had* been the house party.

He'd been one of the rapscallions, always flirting with a different woman, drinking more than he ought to have done, and, in general, behaving as one would expect a rake and a rogue to behave.

Disappointment so bitter Trinity could taste it welled up her throat.

Which was stupid in the extreme.

It made no difference to her if he was a scapegrace. A libertine. A man about town.

"I was." He squinted down at her. "But I do not remember you. At least, I do not think I do."

What a surprise.

He had been too busy flirting with the perfumed and pampered ladies of the *ton*.

He gave her another cockeyed grin. "Surely, I would remember *you*."

Except, when he had first boarded the *Daunting Duchess*, he had reacted as if he did recognize her.

"I shall take over, Miss Ablethorne."

Mr. Compton strode forward, not the least benevolent in demeanor. A severe scowl creased his forehead, and disapproving lines bracketed his firm mouth.

Had Captain Breckett seen her predicament and instructed the second officer to aid her?

"Mr. Everingham should have remained in his cabin if he was such a poor sailor," Mr. Compton said as he traded places with Trinity.

"Sorry about that, old chap." Mr. Everingham offered a weak, apologetic grin. "Never sailed before, you know. Thought the fresh air might help my queasiness."

"I would advise you to stay in your cabin with a slop bucket nearby in the future," Mr. Compton said between clenched teeth with all of the warmth of a coiled viper.

"Aye, aye." Giving the gruff officer an imbecilic grin, Mr. Everingham tried to stand up straight and salute.

His eyes rounded in horror a second before he vomited on Mr. Compton's glossy boots.

4

I have repeatedly told you, Mother, I shall pick my bride when I decide to wed. At six and twenty, I have no compelling desire to trot down the aisle, much less marry into the aristocracy. What's more, I do not give two groats that your grandfather was an earl.

I am a commoner and not ashamed of that fact.

I have left the country to end your meddling once and for all. By week's end, you will have removed yourself to the estate in Essex. There you shall remain until (or if I ever) return to England. I have instructed my man of business to provide you with an adequate allowance, but only if you follow that directive. Should you choose not to, you won't see a half penny. By the by, if you have a mind to live on credit, I have also instructed Shillingford to refuse to pay your bills, and he has notified your creditors and favorite merchants as much.

Galling, isn't it, to be manipulated? Perhaps a taste of your own medicine is what you need to reform your ways and permit me to live my life without your constant, unsolicited interference.

~The rest of Devin Everingham's peeved letter
to his mother, Mrs. Desdemona Everingham
Delivered to their Belgrave house
an hour after he sailed

Three days later
22 October
In his biscuit tin of a cabin

Propped up on three pillows—where Miss Ablethorne had procured the third, he did not know—Devin scraped a palm over his bristly jaw. He bloody well needed a shave. Lifting an arm, he sniffed beneath his arm and grimaced.

God's toes.

A thorough wash would not be amiss, even if the facilities were somewhat lacking.

His movements slow and precise, Devin braced himself for the swell of nausea that did not come. He cautiously stretched his legs beneath the blankets.

Nothing.

Praise God and hallelujah.

He exhaled a hearty sigh of relief.

Had he finally crossed the threshold, and his body had adjusted to the ship's gyrating movements?

Perhaps gyrating was an exaggeration, but the irregular dipping, twisting, swaying, and peaking had taken its toll. And to think, if Devin wanted to follow in his father's footsteps as he'd vowed to do, sailing was very much a part of his future.

That horrific thought nearly sent him diving

beneath the bedclothes with a pillow over his head. *God spare me.*

Mrs. Peagilly swore by her ginger tea. Next time, he would consume the beverage before he set a foot on the wharf.

A full week in advance.

Having awoken several minutes ago, he tried to gauge the time from the sounds filtering below from overhead. No porthole graced his cabin, so he either must open the door or light the candle in the lamp attached to the wall if he wanted to see anything more than dark shadows. He'd been reluctant to do either because that had meant moving. He would rather lie in the dark than risk upsetting his calm stomach.

But now that he appeared to be better, he should haul his sorry arse from his rumpled berth and see to his morning ablutions. He ran his tongue over his teeth and grimaced again. His mouth felt and tasted as if a herd of swine had wallowed inside for a fortnight.

After rising, he steadied himself with a hand braced against the upper berth. It took him a couple of moments to balance and adjust to the ship's tilting.

His empty stomach complained with a low, long rumble.

Hunger, but not queasiness.

No wonder.

He had scarcely eaten since boarding the *Daunting Duchess.*

For the past three days, Miss Ablethorne and Mrs. Peagilly had played nursemaids, bringing him broth and tea, wiping his face with damp cloths, and emptying his slop bucket.

That was beyond mortifying.

Humiliation heated him from waist to hairline, and he squeezed his eyes shut for a heartbeat as the wave receded.

It also galled to have been so incapacitated, and if it had not been for the kindness of the women, Devin was not certain what he would've done.

For certain, Mr. Compton would not have offered to assist again. He had been so furious about Devin casting up his accounts on his perfectly polished boots that he'd ordered two nearby crewmen to see Devin below before he had stomped away, cursing obscenely beneath his breath.

The second officer might very well refuse to speak to Devin for the voyage's duration, which from their brief encounter, was no great loss. Devin consoled himself with the knowledge that by the time he had vomited on Mr. Compton's feet, little remained in his stomach—although he distinctly recalled seeing a speck of chewed carrot.

Regardless, Devin sincerely doubted Compton would perceive the incident in a favorable light.

As Trinity already knew who he was, Devin had opted not to use the name he had registered to sail under. It mattered not if the other passengers or the crew knew his true identity. The deception had only been to put Mother off the scent, and as that had worked marvelously well, there was no point in continuing the ruse.

In short order, Devin had lit the lamp, stripped, and washed using the sandalwood and cedar soap Shillingford had packed. The man was nothing if not detail-oriented. The water in the pitcher was cold but refreshing as Devin poured it over his head. Once he toweled dry, he donned a fresh pair of pantaloons, cleansed his teeth, then proceeded to lather his face for a much-needed shave.

A soft rap preceded the door flying open, and Miss Ablethorne swept in carrying a tray, leaving the door ajar behind her.

"Good morning," she cheerily greeted as was her wont. "I hope you are—"

She gasped as Devin spun toward her bare-chested and with his silver razor in hand.

"You are out of bed," she stated needlessly, her pretty eyes dual moons in her face. She swiftly dropped her gaze to the floor. "I beg your pardon for barging in without permission."

Adorable pink glazed her cheeks as she deftly lowered the panel that sufficed for a table with one hand while balancing the tray with the other. A frown puckered the alabaster contours of her face.

"I brought you gruel, dry toast, and black tea, but perhaps you would prefer something heartier?" Confusion and chagrin puckered her forehead. "Or mayhap you wish to eat in the saloon with the others?"

No, Devin would much rather enjoy a forbidden tête-à-tête with her.

"Gruel and toast are just fine." He was not sure he could stomach anything richer, truth be told.

A pleased smile teased the corners of her mouth before she wrested it under control.

"Hopefully, your constitution will be similar to mine."

At his quirked eyebrow, she continued.

"I was just as wretchedly ill as you on my first voyage." She gave a delicate shudder. "I truly wanted to die."

He well knew that feeling.

"But once I recovered, I have never been plagued with malaise since."

"Never?" Could it be true?

"Never." She rubbed the tip of her nose. "But others become ill with each journey, so I know my circumstance may not be typical."

"I shall pray I am as fortunate as you, Miss Ablethorne."

Even with the door ajar, her presence in a male passenger's quarters, let alone a known rogue's cabin, bordered on scandalous.

Upon waking, Devin had believed it very early morn but now wondered if perhaps it wasn't closer to midmorning.

"Do you know the time, Miss Ablethorne?"

His timepiece was around here someplace. He was not sure where they'd tucked the watch before bundling him into his berth.

"Near ten." She pointed to a peg beside the doorjamb. "That reminds me. Your watch is in your jacket pocket."

"Ah, I wondered where it had gone to."

Trinity swept him a sideways glance from beneath the dark fringe of lashes framing her pale blue eyes. Tied back by a pink ribbon, her wealth of shiny hair hung down her back.

Devin curled his free hand into a ball against the urge to tangle his fingers, or his face, in the satiny curtain.

The pretty pink calico gown she wore, covered with a woolen cherry-toned spencer, edged in matching braid and fastened down the front, suited her far better than the insipid slate affair she'd worn the previous three days.

In short, she was utterly fetching and a welcome breath of fresh air in his stale cabin.

Devin did not miss how her curious gaze skidded over his chest and shoulders, then followed the trail of dark, curly hair to his waistband. A healthy, virile male, he could not help the primal satisfaction that sluiced through him at her covert feminine inspection.

Nevertheless, he snatched a towel and draped it around his shoulders. It was wholly inadequate, but he could not pull his clean shirt over his lathered face. He lifted the razor.

"I shall try the gruel when I have finished shaving. I do not want to overtask my stomach just yet."

Nodding, she edged toward the door.

"Where is Mrs. Peagilly?" he asked, reluctant to have Trinity leave so soon, despite the impropriety of her staying.

For decorum's sake, the widow had always accompanied Miss Ablethorne to his cabin.

"The poor dear awoke with a megrim. Mrs. Peagilly says they are rare for her, but they leave her bedridden

49

until they pass. She says something to do with the atmospheric pressure brought the vile thing on."

Devin gave her a side-eyed glance. "You have not been her companion for a long while?"

Trinity shook her head.

"Only a week. I was a traveling companion to a dear woman for several years. When the opportunity arose to travel again, I applied for the position. This is our first voyage together. We shan't return to England for over a year. Mrs. Peagilly has our itinerary planned. Quite honestly, I am not sure where we are going or who our contacts are."

She gave a little self-conscious laugh.

"Ah, I see. And you enjoy traveling to all sorts of new places? Do you not miss your family?"

"I do enjoy traveling, and I am an orphan." She quirked her brow and gave that little shrug he had come to know as hers. "I think myself fortunate, and I am grateful. There are far fewer desirable positions for a young woman."

She stopped, appearing a trifle chagrined at speaking so freely.

How extraordinary.

Orphaned with no family, compelled to work for her existence, and she believed herself fortunate? Miss Trinity Ablethorne was quite the most intriguing woman he'd ever met.

Biting her lower lip, Trinity shot a glance behind her into the vacant passageway. "I must return to Mrs. Peagilly. She looked most unwell. Feeble even. I confess, I am quite worried about her. I suggested the ship's surgeon see her, but she scoffed at my concern."

"You have missed your calling, Miss Ablethorne. You have a propensity for nursing."

Shaking her head, she wrinkled her nose. "I thank you for your kind words and confidence, but nursing is not my calling. I do not mind tending to someone who is ill, but I cannot abide the sight of blood, gashes, or other wounds. I fear I might swoon, and I heartily despise female theatrics."

"As do I."

A woman possessing common sense and lacking artifice?

Would wonders never cease?

Lifting an eyebrow, Devin gave her a cocky grin before turning his attention to the small mirror.

"Swoon?" He paused in scraping the razor across his jaw to view her in the mirror. "I have not known you long, Miss Ablethorne, but you do not strike me as the sort of young lady who faints."

"True, I have not as yet." *Ah, there it is.* "And I do pride myself on being stoic." Head canted, she fiddled with the braid at her cuff, then shrugged. "But everyone has their weaknesses and flaws. Yes?"

"Indeed."

And his, at this precise moment, was an unwise, certain-to-be-trouble mounting interest in the pretty miss.

Devin turned his attention to the tricky area on his chin to distract himself from his wayward, ever-increasing carnal musings.

"Miss Ablethorne, would you care to stroll on the deck after you have looked in on Mrs. Peagilly and I have finished dressing and breaking my fast?"

"That would be lovely—"

His pulse accelerated in anticipation of spending more time with her in, if not precisely a romantic environment, a setting more appealing than a sick room where the faint odor of vomit yet lingered.

"But rain has deluged the vessel for two and a half days. It is not fit for man or beast top side. I pity the sailors, though most wear oilskin and seem to take the rainstorm in stride." Trinity swept her full plum-colored lips upward in a sweetly contrite smile. "I have taken to pacing the passageway for a bit of exercise, inadequate though it is."

Such an overwhelming urge to kiss those two plump pillows and the adorable dimple in Trinity's buttercup of a chin battered Devin that he nearly spun around, grabbed her to his naked chest, and plundered the depths of that oh-so-tempting mouth.

No.

NO, he repeated more firmly in his head.

He had committed to putting his roguish ways behind him and becoming the man his father always believed he could be.

A gentleman. An honorable man. A man his father would be proud to call his son.

Razor poised at his jaw, Devin swallowed, then swallowed again.

"Chess then? In the saloon?"

To keep appearances perfectly respectable.

"Regretfully, I do not play." She notched a shoulder upward an inch, not the least apologetic.

Devil take it.

"I could teach you."

"You could try. However, I have undertaken to learn the game but found it not to my liking. I lack the competitiveness needed to prevail. I do not care if my opponent captures my priests, knights, crows, pawns, or queen."

She sent another surreptitious glance over her shoulder.

Devin could not contain his chuckle. "You mean bishop and rook?"

Nonplussed, she stared at him. "Pardon?"

"Not priests but bishops, and not crows but rooks." He waved his razor. "And those names are the English versions. Rook is from *rukh,* which means chariot, and the bishop was originally *alfil* for elephant."

Arms folded, she slanted a delicate eyebrow upward.

"Now you are making a May game of me."

"Not at all." He shook his head, and a blob of lather plopped onto the scuffed floor.

"Chess originated in India. The pieces were named for the four army divisions. Infantry, or what we call pawns."

He raised his forefinger.

"Calvary, the knights. The elephantry is the bishops because a small groove on the pieces is supposed to represent a tusk."

He lifted two more lathered fingers.

"And the chariotry became rooks."

He pointed a fourth finger ceilingward.

Misgiving narrowed Trinity's eyes, and she tapped the toes of one foot. "What about the king and queen?"

Devin applied the razor to his neck before rinsing it in the basin.

"The king was always king or *Rajah*, and the queen was originally *Mantri* which means advisor. After chess reached Europe, the advisor piece changed to the queen."

"Why do you know so much about chess?" Trinity sounded unconvinced.

"My father adored the game. He brought me a set from India many years ago." Devin pointed to the low trunk. "It is in there. He also shared the game's history that he learned while in India."

"And that is why you love the game too."

Nodding, Devin let his mind travel back to the last chess game he ever played with Father. He had been sober that night for a change.

The next day, he lay dead at the bottom of the stairs. Two empty whisky bottles told the tale. Reeling drunk, he'd fallen and broken his neck.

Devin eyed Trinity's reflection in the mirror. She really ought to have gone several minutes ago. Detaining her jeopardized her reputation and possibly her standing with her employer.

He truly was a selfish cad.

"Thank you for sharing those fascinating tidbits with me." She pushed several strands of hair off her shoulders. "Mayhap I shall try to learn it again."

She made to go.

"What about checkers?" Devin blurted.

Was there a set on board the vessel?

Amongst the crew, perchance?

Devin had asked Shillingford to pack his chess set

and playing cards but not checkers.

Trinity gave her head a remorseful shake, sending the hair caressing her back swaying. "I am simply dismal at most games, from shuttlecock to pall mall to hazard."

A spark lit her azure eyes, and she grinned.

"Except for piquet or vingt-et-un. I play both satisfactorily." She rearranged his eating utensils to her satisfaction, then with a precocious upward sweep of that tempting mouth, asked, "Do you play either, Mr. Everingham?"

Was that sincere interest causing the huskiness in her voice or something else?

Preferring whist or faro, Devin nevertheless nodded his head. "I do indeed, and my cards are in one of those."

So were his dice.

He nudged his chin toward the two closed trunks.

"Excellent." Trinity clasped her hands, her gaze flitting around the tiny chamber but studiously avoiding settling on him.

She cleared her throat.

"Well then, Mr. Everingham, I shall leave you to…"

Waving a hand in his general direction, she took a step backward.

"*Miss Ablethorne?*"

56

5

I hope this letter finds you in excellent health, lady. I regret to inform you that a fire ravaged the hotel last month and your usual rooms were destroyed. There is much sickness in the city, and I encourage you to delay your visit. Even your guide, Kadeen Aziz, has fallen ill.
Stay home, lady, until springtime.
I shall write you when it is safe.

Zarif Yassine, Concierge of Riad Les Zarabel,
in a letter to Mrs. Eustacia Peagilly
Sent but never received

Still in Devin's cabin
Five very uncomfortable seconds later

A female's shocked exclamation, her voice pitching earsplitting high on the last syllable, yanked Devin's and Trinity's attention to the narrow, dimly lit passage.

Ah, bloody—

A woman wearing a neat royal blue traveling ensemble and holding the hands of a little boy and girl, obviously her progeny, gaped, eyes round as saucers and mouth slack as a dead trout.

"Good morning, Mrs. McKinnick." Seemingly

unaffected, Trinity slipped from Devin's chamber. "Hello, Georgie. Gladys."

"Mama, why can we not go up on deck?" the petulant little girl demanded before frowning and pointing at Devin. "Why doesn't that man have a shirt on?"

"'Cause you cannot shave with a shiwt on, silly," the little chap—looking quite dapper in his cranberry-colored skeleton suit—stated matter-of-factly before jamming his thumb back into his mouth. He pulled it out halfway and craned his neck to look at his mother.

"Can I pway swowds?" he mumbled around his thumb.

"Not now, Georgie," his frazzled mother replied distractedly.

"But I want to pway piwate," Georgie insisted. "I shall be Black Beawd."

What little boy would not want to pretend to be a famous pirate on a sailing ship?

His older sister pursed her lips, rolled her eyes, and shook her head, causing her coppery ringlets to pirouette.

"Pi-rr-ates"—she deliberately emphasized the 'r' sound her brother struggled to pronounce—"do not suck their thumbs, dummy."

"Gladys, do not call your brother names," her

58

mother tiredly reprimanded. She narrowed her eyes. "Dear, your spencer is not buttoned correctly."

Sure enough, Gladys had mismatched the buttons on her fern-green velvet spencer.

Georgie grinned around the thumb in his mouth, and his sister stuck her tongue out at him as she bent to setting her buttons aright.

Trinity angled toward Devin.

"You have been quite ill, Mr. Everingham. Do not try to eat all of the breakfast I brought you. You would be better off nibbling a portion now and then eating a bit more in an hour or so. Sample small servings throughout the day to help you recover your strength but not overtax your digestive system."

She did not seem the least affected or embarrassed by Mrs. McKinnick's judgmental stare.

"If you will please excuse me. I must check on Mrs. Peagilly." Trinity touched her temple. "She has a nasty headache which kept her abed this morning."

That triggered an empathetic reaction from the offended woman.

"The poor dear. I have headache powders and smelling salts should Mrs. Peagilly need them." Mrs. McKinnick glanced downward at her auburn-haired children. "I am prone to sick headaches myself. In truth, I feel one niggling behind my eyes even now."

No doubt, being stuck in a cabin with her energetic children contributed to her discomfort.

"I am so sorry you are ailing. Thank you for your kind offer of headache powders, but Mrs. Peagilly took a dose earlier." Trinity glanced between Gladys and Georgie. "Allow me to make sure she doesn't require anything, and perhaps the children might join Mr. Everingham and me in the saloon. We are going to play cards, but I am sure we could think of a game or two for the children while you have a lie-down."

Mrs. McKinnick blinked owlishly.

"You would...?" She delicately cleared her throat. "You would truly do that?"

A smile blossomed across Trinity's face, softening the corners in kindness and compassion. She was not beautiful in the classic sense, nor did she possess the popular pale blonde locks favored by the *haut ton*.

Regardless, Devin's breath caught in his lungs, and a weird sensation tugged behind his ribs. What about this woman intrigued him like no other ever had?

For nigh on a decade, he'd had his pick of gorgeous, alluring women. Yet, this unassuming companion had him discarding protocols, common sense, and his self-imposed strictures with the abandonment of tippler who'd downed too many ales.

"Indeed," Trinity said, no guile in her clear blue

eyes. "If the children and Mr. Everingham are willing, that is."

"Can we, Mama?" Gladys bounced on her toes. "Can we, *ple-ee-ase*?"

The child drew out the word into several syllables in a toe-curling, wheedling whine.

"Do you know how to play swowds?" Georgie asked Devin matter-of-factly, holding his puckered thumb at the ready to stuff back into his mouth.

Devin had swiftly finished shaving, dried his face, and donned a shirt. "I believe I can manage a decent battle with blades should I be required to defend a lady's honor against a notorious pirate."

A smile tugging the corners of his mouth upward, he struck a fencing pose.

Georgie looked at his Mama and gave a solemn nod, one more befitting a magistrate.

"I agree, Mama."

Devin bit back a bark of laughter.

"Thank you, Miss Ablethorne." Mrs. McKinnick managed a wan smile. "I gladly accept your generous offer. I am in the family way again, and I have not adjusted to sleeping on the ship."

"Splendid." Trinity winked at Devin, and he grinned. "I shall be but a few minutes. I shall meet all of you in the saloon."

She disappeared into another cabin as Mrs. McKinnick ushered her children along the passage toward the largest chamber aboard the ship.

Well, I'll be tarred and feathered.

Somehow, Trinity had wrangled Devin into the role of a nanny, and he did not mind in the least—if it meant spending time with a certain young lady.

Be careful, a wise, cautionary inner voice warned.

What was there to fret about?

He had anticipated a shipboard flirtation as a distraction and a source of entertainment, and it was not merely male arrogance that made him confident Miss Ablethorne was not immune to him.

Her curious blue gaze roving over his bare shoulders and chest attested to her interest.

What could go wrong?

6

You are aware that I am not like many of my girlhood friends. I have never possessed a driving need to discover my origins, nor have I centered my life around the hope of marriage and a family. I believe it paramount that we accept what we cannot change and pursue what we can if it is our heart's desire. How often did you quote scripture, reminding us that the Lord knows his plans for us? To prosper us and not to harm us, and to give us hope and a future?

I shall admit to finding that difficult to believe at times, but hope is an enduring force. It empowers, energizes, and above all, equips me with optimism. I truly enjoy being a companion and traveling the world. When I consider the alternatives for a discarded child of unknown origins, I cannot help but be grateful that someone—though I likely shall never know who—chose to place me at Haven House and Academy for the Enrichment of Young Women.

I cannot contend that had I been born a male, my circumstances would have been any better, except for the basic rights men take for granted. So I accept my fate and seize each opportunity as it arises. The resulting memories shall inspire me in my loneliness when I am old, frail, and feeble.

I shall endeavor to find a keepsake to bring back to you. Perhaps something from Morocco.

~Miss Trinity Ablethorne,
in a letter to Mrs. Hester Shepherd,
the proprietress of Haven House
and Academy for the Enrichment of Young Women

Daunting Duchess's saloon— a not very large, crowded cabin
Three hours later

Out of habit, Trinity tapped her chin with the end of her pencil as she regarded the sketch of Devin and Georgie. Legs crossed as if he were a lad himself, Devin sat on the floor, playing soldiers with the little fellow, who had tired of sword fighting some time ago.

Gladys and two of her dollies occupied a corner where an elaborate tea party with Lady Jersey and Queen Charlotte in attendance commenced.

Bearing toys for his children, Sir Godfrey had popped in an hour ago to check on his son and daughter. His wife, he explained, slept soundly, and he loathed disturbing her. When assured the children were no bother and that Trinity was happy to continue watching them, he thanked her profusely.

He needed to review documents for his new diplomatic assignment and would welcome uninterrupted quiet.

When she'd checked on Mrs. Peagilly before coming to the saloon, the dear woman had been pale and weak but maintained all she needed was to sleep in a completely dark cabin in utter silence. She had insisted that Trinity avail herself of the saloon and that she needn't rush to return. It usually took four and twenty hours for Mrs. Peagilly to recover fully from one of her megrims.

Still, Trinity could not help but feel a trifle guilty, but what was she to do in a dark cabin? Nonetheless, she intended to peek in on her employer to ensure Mrs. Peagilly rested comfortably before making herself scarce again.

Misters Truman-Shelton and Meriwether sat shoulder to shoulder and heads together at the other end of the well-used table, pouring over ledgers and conversing in low tones. From time to time, one would glance up befuddled and appear almost puzzled that anyone else also occupied the paneled saloon.

As they had every time Trinity encountered the men, they wore almost identical charcoal gray suits, the one notable difference being their cravats. Mr. Truman-Shelton's was a simple knot, while Mr. Meriwether's neckcloth boasted a complicated waterfall Beau Brummel would've envied.

Given the lack of laundry facilities on the ship, that starched masterpiece would eventually become a limp, wilted shadow of what it now was.

Though the saloon acted as the dining quarters and a gathering area for passengers and ranking crew members, functionality was at the forefront of its design.

With her fingertip, Trinity traced a two-inch scratch on the long table, which dominated the cabin's center. Scarred and scuffed from years of usage, like the other large pieces of furniture, metal strips held in place by nails anchored it to the floor.

A walnut sideboard for serving food took up most of one wall and scraped and scratched extra chairs took up the other. Two dusty lanterns, their sooty glass panes in need of a good scrub, hung from hooks over the table, and a faded blue tufted bench resided beneath the single porthole, atop which slept the ship's cat, Duchess, her nose tucked beneath her fluffy tail.

In addition to conveying a limited number of passengers to various destinations, the *Daunting Duchess* mainly transported goods.

Trinity had learned those details from Mr. Alderton during supper last night. The man spoke of the ship with great affection, giving credence to the saying that a ship and the sea were tantalizing mistresses to some men.

The promised game of cards with Devin had not begun yet, but Trinity did not mind. She enjoyed watching his interactions with the children. Mayhap he had nieces and nephews in England and had acquired his patience and kindness from having spent time with them.

She had never had the opportunity to be around

children. She liked them well enough but was not as skilled with little ones as were her friends Mercy, Chasity, and Purity, all of whom had either worked as governesses or instructors.

Trinity's tummy growled, reminding her she'd only eaten a couple of spoonfuls of porridge this morning. In truth, she detested porridge, but one could not be picky at sea, where the fare was often limited. Particularly on merchant ships that did not cater to different classes of passengers.

It must be near the time for the midday meal, and she hoped for more palatable fare to fill her complaining stomach. Even stew and bread would suffice.

Mr. Everingham really ought to have eaten something before now too. Guilt pricked her because had she not invited him to join her and the children in the saloon, he would've been able to pick at his breakfast tray at his leisure.

The door creaked open, and a much-refreshed Mrs. McKinnick swept in.

"Mama," cried Georgie, holding up two tin soldiers and grinning. "I won the battle."

That his thumb was not stuck in his mouth and had not been for the better part of an hour said much about how much fun he was having.

"That is wonderful, dear." His mother gave him a

preoccupied smile as she sought the whereabouts of her other offspring. Upon spying Gladys holding an imaginary cup to her mouth—pinky extended—she visibly relaxed.

Trinity closed her sketchpad and placed her pencils back into their holder.

Georgie sent Devin a consolatory glance. "Mr. Everingham is not vewy good at waw, but he showed me a few satisfactowy fencing moves."

All was forgiven it seemed.

Devin's well-practiced fencing poses earned him clemency for his lack of warfare strategies. A pair of rolled up news sheets had sufficed as foils. Even Gladys had tried her hand at a few maneuvers—only after Trinity assured her many girls were adept at the sport, and her mama would not object because it wasn't ladylike.

Trinity, however, begged off a lesson, all too conscious of the other two men crouched at the other end of the table. It was one thing for a little girl to prance and pose with a pretend sword and another thing altogether for a grown woman. Though, truth be told, she would not mind learning the sport.

"Put your soldiers away, darling." Mrs. McKinnick said. "The rain has stopped, and Papa wants to take a turn on deck and stretch his legs before we eat luncheon."

Devin helped Georgie gather his soldiers and place them in the tin. After he rose and brushed off his knees, Devin joined Trinity at the table.

His warm dark brown eyes twinkled with amusement.

Was he ever surly or cross?

Even at his sickest—and he had been deucedly ill—he'd maintained a kindly air.

Pathetically weak and pitiful but kind.

He had not protested at being corralled into being a nursemaid for children he did not know either. For a reason Trinity could not quite put her finger on, that compensated for his roguish behavior at the Mumford's last summer. A very tiny compensation and one that did not wholly redeem him, but an improvement in his status from rakehell to rogue, nonetheless.

"I should like to stretch my legs as well," Devin said, helping himself to an apple from a bowl in the center of the table. He must be famished, yet he had not grumbled a jot. "Might I persuade you to join me, Miss Ablethorne?"

Yes, he might.

But before Trinity answered, he added, "Perhaps Mrs. Peagilly is feeling up to a bit of exercise as well?"

He bit into the apple with a satisfactory crunch.

"I know I am," Mr. Truman-Shelton said as he

stretched his arms wide and arched his back—his spine rendering a popping crack—before he gathered his papers into a sloppy stack.

"Me too," agreed his business associate. Mr. Meriwether also scooped several documents and ledgers together. "Although, I would like to discuss a business proposition with you when it is convenient, Mr. Everingham."

His mouth full of apple, Devin merely arched a quizzical eyebrow.

Scratching his nape, Mr. Meriwether gave a sheepish grin. "It is no secret you are a partial owner of the *Daunting Duchess* and that you inherited your father's business enterprises. We"—he veered his business associate a swift glance to include him— "believe we have an opportunity that would be advantageous to all of us."

He slid his comrade another indecipherable look.

"Erm, yes." Mr. Truman-Shelton nodded, slightly taken aback. He ran a finger along the edge of his neckcloth in a decidedly nervous fashion. He recovered quickly, schooling his face into a bland mask. "Yes. Yes, indeed. A most advantageous proposition, if I do say so myself. Which I do, of course. Otherwise, why mention it, aye?"

Mr. Meriwether speared him a shut-up-for-god's-sake scowl.

His Adam's apple jiggling his cravat like a mouse scurrying up and down, Mr. Truman-Shelton gulped and meshed his lips together.

Trinity eyed the pair, taking in their neat suits and polished but well-worn shoes.

Something was not as it seemed about those two.

She would wager on it.

Devin's other eyebrow crept up minutely as he regarded the men and chewed happily on another bite of his apple. He swallowed. "I am sure we shall find an opportunity for a discussion on the voyage."

Oh, very clever.

Well done, you.

His polite response was not a precise agreement, and from the contemplative look he leveled Meriwether and Truman-Shelton, Trinity surmised he was not taken in by their friendly gesture either.

Good to know Trinity was not the only one suspicious of the oily pair.

Just how had they come to know Devin was a partial owner?

Trinity had not mentioned it—not even to Mrs. Peagilly.

That meant a member of the crew had loose lips.

Devin turned the apple to the uneaten side before leveling the men a contemplative glance. "I presume that if this venture is outside of Britain, you have researched the laws and customs of the country or countries where the enterprise is to take place? Failure to do so can prove calamitous or worse."

His focus fixed on the floor, a gray-green cast came over Mr. Truman-Shelton's face while Mr. Meriwether nodded and harumphed. "Of course. Indeed."

Gladys, holding a doll under each arm, approached. "Esmerelda-Marigold and Felicity-Elizabeth could use a breath of fresh air too."

Trinity had no idea which doll was which.

"Thank Miss Ablethorne and Mr. Everingham, children," their mother instructed. That she had not foisted her children off to a nursemaid or governess spoke well of her maternal instincts, for surely a diplomat could afford to hire a servant to assist with Gladys and Georgie.

"Thank you," the children chimed in unison.

"You are very welcome." Trinity glanced at Devin and slanted her eyes meaningfully toward the little boy and girl.

He bent into a formal bow. "It was my pleasure Master McKinnick, Miss McKinnick."

Gladys giggled and whispered something to her dollies that sounded very much like, "Isn't he handsome?"

Georgie scowled at his sister and then extended his small hand in a manner he must've seen his father do, which Devin promptly shook.

"I shall pwactice my fencing." Georgie puffed out his chest like a proud bantam rooster.

His sister stuck her tongue out at him again.

Mrs. McKinnick passed Trinity two small brown paper bags. "For you and Mr. Everingham. Lemon and licorice drops. I always keep a generous supply on hand. Sir Godfrey and I both have a fondness for sweets, and they help soothe my stomach as well."

She probably used them to bribe her children too.

"Thank you." Trinity rarely had the opportunity to indulge in sweets.

"I hope I shall see you on deck." Her face wreathed in a smile, Mrs. McKinnick shooed her children before her.

Mr. Truman-Shelton and Mr. Meriwether followed in her wake. At the door, Mr. Meriwether glanced over his shoulder toward Devin, speculation in his eyes.

Devin finished eating the fruit, tossed the core into a rubbish bin in the corner, and selected another apple.

Trinity opened the first bag and peeked inside. She inhaled the candy's essence before selecting a licorice and popping it into her mouth.

Utterly delicious.

She extended the bag toward Devin.

"Licorice drop, Devin?"

Grinning, he waggled his eyebrows and helped himself to a tasty nugget.

"Did you just address me by my given name, *Trinity*?"

Taken aback because his name had flowed from her lips so readily, Trinity's mouth dropped open.

"Why, yes. Yes, I did. I beg your pardon. I am not sure what came over me."

Mirth lighting Devin's eyes—he had such lovely, warm, melted chocolate eyes—he dropped his candy into his mouth. He leaned nearer and winked.

"I do not mind."

Heat seared Trinity's cheeks.

She'd best be more careful, or he would think her fast.

Hadn't he said she was forward already?

Yes.

When she had helped him that first night.

Rogues like him would think nothing of a shipboard tryst, especially if he believed her a willing participant.

She, on the other hand, had her reputation to consider.

Mrs. Peagilly might not be conventional according to *le beau monde* standards, but even she mightn't approve of her new companion compromising her reputation—even unintentionally.

"Well, *I* do mind." Trinity lifted her chin in a show of determination and defiance, which would've been more effective if her chin did not possess a small dimple. Others found the indentation charming, but she'd always thought it made her appear weak. "Such familiarity is not proper."

"Neither was your entering my chamber this morning," Devin said without a jot of remorse or a moment's hesitation.

He was right; dash it all.

Must he be so smug about it though?

"Well, as I said previously, Mr. Everingham, circumstances sometimes prevent adherence to social strictures aboard a ship. However, when protocols can be observed, they should be."

Trinity hid a grimace.

She sounded as prim as a fusty old maid.

"Will you stroll with me?" Devin neatly changed the subject and took the wind from her sails in the process.

"After I look in on Mrs. Peagilly." She nodded. "If she doesn't need me, I shall meet you."

Trinity had neglected her employer all morning and would not be surprised if Mrs. Peagilly required her services for the remainder of the day. After all, she was not employing her to watch other people's children or take the air with handsome rapscallions.

Devin took her hand and raised it to his lips.

She should object—yank her hand away.

Scold Devin for overstepping.

But her will seemed to have flittered away, along with what remained of her common sense. In truth, she wanted him to kiss her hand. With her breath suspended, she anticipated the touch with far more eagerness than was warranted.

He brushed those velvety lips across her skin, the merest whisp of a touch. Which could in no way account for the acceleration of her pulse, the tingling from knee to neck, or the blood heating in her veins.

Could it?

Mouth parted, she stared at him, slightly dazed.

He lowered his eyelids over his smoldering gaze, and good thing too, for she was nigh on to going up in a conflagration of sensation.

Did he feel it too?

"Until then, little prude."

"Pru…prude?" she stuttered on an unbecoming squeak, coming back to herself with a jolt. "I am *not* a prude."

Compared to the women whose company he

normally shared, she must appear as prim and proper as a nun. Except, she had been unchaperoned in his cabin when he was dishabille.

Had he forgotten that?

Laughing, he winked, tossed the apple in the air before catching it and taking a bite, and then strode from the saloon.

Good Lord.

Devin Everingham was dangerous. Perilous to a spinster with no experience in warding off disarming rogues. What was more, Trinity was not altogether certain she wanted to discourage him.

I have much to tell you but am too distraught at present. Forgive me for the briefness of my note. I shall write again when I am able. I must pen a note to Vicar Howard and share the unfortunate news, though it will be a week before I can post the letter and at least another week before it reaches England.

I wish you were here. I would not feel so very alone and uncertain.

~Miss Trinity Ablethorne, in a short missive
to her friend, Mrs. Faith Kellinggrave
Never posted

Near ten of the clock that evening
Daunting Duchess's poop deck

Trinity did not join Devin for a walk, nor did she appear in the saloon for dinner. Mrs. Peagilly had not improved but worsened to such an extent that an hour ago, Captain Breckett had sent the ship's surgeon, Will Morris, to tend the ill woman.

Hopefully, whatever ailed her would pass soon, and she and Trinity could enjoy the rest of the short voyage in anticipation of their time in Morocco and beyond. Devin did not know what brought Mrs. Peagilly to the

Mediterranean, and Trinity had not mentioned it either.

Perchance she did not know.

After all, a mere companion mightn't have her employer's confidence, particularly a new employer. Although, Mrs. Peagilly did not seem the sort to stand on formality and pretentiousness.

Devin planned on meeting with Father's leather suppliers at the tannery in Fez. The leather, amongst the softest and most pliable available anywhere, could be dyed into rich, vibrant shades, ideal for book bindings as well as ladies' gloves and slippers.

Resting his elbows on the rail, Devin breathed in the tangy, salty air and contemplated the wake the ship carved through the ocean as the winds carried her ever closer to Spain and into the Straights of Gibraltar.

He'd always been content in England, never having a great desire to see the world, but this venture, though only beginning, gave him a greater appreciation for travel—less the gut-wrenching sickness that had plagued him, of course. Perhaps he had inherited more of his father's wanderlust spirit than he realized or acknowledged.

Mother would have a conniption fit when she learned he intended frequent and possibly lengthy travels from here on out. In truth, he had no immediate plans to return to England.

Mayhap not for a year or two.

After finishing his business in Fez, he wanted to tour Greece before journeying onward to India. He raised his face to the heavens, welcoming the breeze and ocean spray.

There was something glorious, almost spiritual, about being on the vessel in the middle of the Atlantic Ocean. They were mere playthings, reliant upon the fickle winds' whims to convey them to another continent. To a degree, he had begun to understand his father's love of traveling—something Father had relinquished toward the end of his life because Mother had demanded it.

Though not quite back to normal, Devin's stomach had calmed sufficiently to permit him to eat modest amounts of bland food and move about the ship at will. More than once, his wandering feet had led him to the rectangular opening leading to below deck. He'd turned around and strode to another portion of the ship each time.

What did he intend?

To stand sentry outside Mrs. Peagilly and Trinity's cabin?

There was nothing he could do for Mrs. Peagilly or Trinity. He had no inclination to sip brandy in the saloon, particularly since the first officer had returned to duty some five and forty minutes ago, and Mr. Compton had gone below for dinner.

The man pointedly rebuffed Devin when they encountered each other on deck this afternoon. It was not as if this were London, where one could go years without seeing someone. Unless Devin confined himself to his cabin, he and Compton would come across each other.

The man behaved like a sullen child.

Thumb-sucking Georgie possessed more maturity and civility than the second officer, whose boots appeared no worse for the wear from the unfortunate incident a few nights ago.

Half-turning, Devin perused the sailors on deck.

Had one of those poor sots been assigned to clean Compton's boots?

He would wager his precious chess set that the officer had not dirtied his hands with the task himself.

While gruff and a man of few words, Captain Breckett was fair and well-respected. The first officer, Mr. Alderton, could only sing the ship's praises, her exceptional speed, majesty, and so on, and he was beloved by the crew. However, the same could not be said of Compton, full of self-importance and condescending to all but the captain and first officer.

In the few hours he'd been topside, Devin had

observed more than one sailor sending a glare, scowl, or vulgar gesture toward the second mate's back. A few had directed sizzling oaths at the man under their breath.

No, the crew did not adore Mr. Thaddeus Compton.

Tapping his fingertips on the polished rail, Devin permitted a sardonic grin.

Could he have Mr. Compton dismissed if Devin requested it?

Now that was a tempting notion.

Regardless, he would not exploit his position. That would make him as much of an arse as Compton. It would surprise him if Captain Breckett gave the arrogant blighter his *congé*. This ship was not a naval vessel where a commission could be bought and sold almost as easily as a flip of a coin or the right hands greased with a few extra coins.

These sailors, and presumably Compton too, were hired on merit, experience, and skill.

The dulcet, haunting tones of a medieval vessel flute floated on the crisp air. Devin stretched his neck to identify who played the unusual instrument. He was familiar with the globular flute because he possessed one—another treasure from his father from one of his many voyages abroad. Devin's lay tucked into a soft, etched leather case in his trunk below.

He had come upon his flute today when he'd

searched for a book to read to pass the time after learning Trinity would not be joining him. He had eschewed reading in his cabin in exchange for the bracing salt air. It would either quicken his recovery or send him to an early grave.

He roved his gaze over the various decks. Muted lantern light caused the shadows to sway and dance in unison with the ship's movements.

There, near the foredeck.

A man, possibly a Moroccan, with pitch-black hair, nut-brown skin, and wearing a burgundy striped djellaba over loose black pants, sat cross-legged, his eyes closed as he played a clay instrument. The soothing unfamiliar melody filled the air before drifting away on the breeze.

Devin would have to find the sailor later, and perhaps they could play together.

Strange how he, accustomed to crowds of people surrounding him at parties, assemblies, routs, and the like, stood alone on this ship, yet he wasn't lonely. In point of fact, an undefinable contentment enshrouded him.

Still, he was not eager to return to his cramped cabin just yet.

Three days of his own company in the windowless, small space proved more than enough, thank you very much. Until now, he had not known he had an aversion to close quarters. But then again, until this voyage, he had never been in such a confined space for days on end either.

This time of night, none of the other passengers remained above deck.

The McKinnicks had retired to their cabins for the night, and he presumed Meriwether and Truman-Shelton were ensconced in the saloon plotting whatever the pair schemed.

Devin did not trust them.

They were too slick, too pleasant, too accommodating.

If he'd learned one lesson from his father, it was how to spot an unscrupulous charlatan. Whatever the businessmen were about, he would be bound that it was illegal, immoral, or deceptive—likely all three. He meant to keep an eye on them, and if they approached anyone else about their investment opportunity, he would speak a word of caution in the would-be victim's ear.

Tugging on his earlobe, he turned his attention back to the churning water.

Earlier today, Captain Breckett said they could expect the weather to warm as they sailed southward. A less severe cold had already replaced that first night's biting, bone-penetrating chill. A couple more days, the captain assured Devin, and he would shed his cloak and greatcoat.

"Mr. Everingham? A word, if you please."

Deep in his thoughts and with the waves crashing against the hull, Devin had not heard the captain's heavy-gaited approach.

"Yes, Captain?"

Grooves from decades of sun and wind exposure etched Captain Breckett's weathered face. What was not covered by silvery whiskers, that was. But something more than the elements deepened the grooves around his eyes and across his forehead.

The captain stared at a point beyond Devin's shoulder, his gaze troubled.

"Is something amiss, Captain?"

Did a storm approach?

Devin did not want to contemplate what havoc a tempest could wreak on his constitution.

A swift, wary glance to the horizon revealed nothing suspicious or alarming, but then again, he did not know what to look for in a brewing gale.

Chin tucked to his chest and arms behind his back, the captain gave a severe nod. He took a step nearer and murmured in a subdued tone, "Mr. Morris just informed me that Mrs. Peagilly has passed from this world."

What?

Devin shook his head.

He could not have heard correctly.

Mrs. Peagilly merely had a headache.

He cleared his throat. "Mrs. Peagilly…*died?*"

The captain gave a grave nod. "Sadly so. Massive apoplexy, according to Morris. Nothing could be done. I shall perform the funeral tomorrow morning."

Devin hid a wince.

Mrs. Peagilly would rest on the bottom of the Atlantic for eternity. There was no way to preserve a body for months until the *Daunting Duchess* returned to England. And yet, somehow, that seemed fitting for the adventurous woman.

Trinity.

He snapped his head up.

"Miss Ablethorne?"

"Is distraught but composed. Even now, she prepares Mrs. Peagilly's body."

Who else would do it?

Mrs. McKinnick?

Surely not a sailor.

"Sweet Jesus." Devin clasped his nape. "What is to become of Miss Ablethorne?"

The captain stared at him blankly. "I am afraid I do not take your meaning."

"She was to remain in Mrs. Peagilly's company for at least a year. She doesn't know her employer's itinerary or her contact in Morocco, and I am certain she hasn't enough funds to support herself."

Probably not monies for return passage either.

"You seem to know quite a lot about her." Captain Breckett's expression remained unchanged, yet his voice contained the merest undefinable inflection.

"She and Mrs. Peagilly did attend me for three days while I was ill."

Not that Devin was capable of more than one-or-two-word grunts.

"Hmph." The captain grazed his callused fingers over his beard. "We have a problem then."

"Which is?"

"The passenger quarters are fully booked for the next four ports. Miss Ablethorne cannot return to England on the *Daunting Duchess,* and I cannot in good conscience discharge her, a lone female with no recourse, into a foreign country."

"Surely, there is a single available berth for her?" Devin well understood how dire Trinity's situation was. An unchaperoned English woman was not safe in London, let alone Morocco.

"No, there is not. Many more English are eager to leave Morocco than visit. I have heard there is widespread sickness. I am not permitting my men to go ashore except to unload our cargo." Captain Breckett's intense gaze bore into Devin. "As the ship's owner, the responsibility lies with you to remedy the situation."

"*Me?*" Devin stared at him as if the captain had sprouted another nose. "What can I do?"

He barely knew Trinity and was a stranger to Africa himself. Naturally, his man of affairs had made arrangements in advance for lodgings, an interpreter, and transportation, but those details did not include accommodating a female.

Devin was quite out of his element, and if there were sickness in the city...

Yet, he could not abandon her either.

Trinity had no one—no one but him.

The captain slapped him on the shoulder.

"I am sure you will come up with something." His countenance grew grim. "For her sake, you had better. Fair-skinned, blue-eyed women are valuable on the slave market. Particularly innocents."

Was he saying...?

He could not mean...

Was Trinity in danger of being abducted and sold as a sex slave?

Devin gulped against the surge of bile billowing up his throat.

Not, by God, as long as he drew breath.

8

I am not sure when I shall arrange passage to England, but when I arrive, might I impose upon you for a week or two? Only until I can find a new position, of course. I am loath to be a burden to you and Dr. Morrisette. If it is too inconvenient, please do not hesitate to say so when I arrive. I shall ask Mercy or Chasity instead.

~Miss Trinity Ablethorne, in a letter to her friend,
Mrs. Joy Morrisette
Penned the day after Mrs. Peagilly passed,
then tucked away unfinished

The Daunting Duchess's main deck
Ten the next morning

Numb from shock rather than cold—for in just four days, the weather had warmed dramatically— Trinity stood amongst the other passengers and crew, their heads bowed in respect, as Captain Breckett, also an ordained pastor, read from *The Book of Common Prayer*.

"… O Sovereign Lord Christ, deliver your servant, Eustacia Peagilly…" the captain droned on.

Befuddled and her mind and emotions

overwhelmed with sorrow and confusion, Trinity only half-heard the ceremony.

It had not been a megrim.

What was worse, Trinity had left the poor woman to suffer alone for hours, whiling away the time in the saloon sketching, laughing, playing with children...*and flirting.*

"Almighty God, look with pity upon the sorrows of your servant for whom we pray..."

But Mrs. Peagilly had insisted that Trinity leave the cabin so that she might recover from her megrim in her normal manner. Neither of them could've known how serious her condition was. Nor, according to Mr. Morris, could anything have been done but make her as comfortable as possible.

Which was not saying much, considering they were in the middle of the ocean.

"Yea, though I walk through the valley of the shadow of death..."

Nonetheless, guilt tormented Trinity.

Not just remorse, but worry; for now, what was she to do?

She had received no wages yet, and her meager savings would not even buy her passage back to England. A companion made scarce little. Her employer paid for her room, board, and most other necessities in lieu of wages.

Unless she could find someone needing a companion when they put ashore, she might very well find herself stranded. But how could she survive in a foreign country when she did not speak the language and had no means of supporting herself until she found a position?

She swallowed the painful lump forming in her raw throat.

God above, she hated being at the mercy of others. Especially a thousand miles from home. And she was frightened and, in truth, angry with herself for not considering something tragic might occur on this wild adventure. She should've had a plan. Not that she could have anticipated Mrs. Peagilly dying before they even made it to Morocco, but still.

Trinity ought to have put a little forethought into what she would do in an emergency, and she had not given it a single consideration. That was what came of always being at the mercy of her companion's whims. She never had the opportunity to consider what *she* would do.

The tears she'd shed these past hours had not been entirely for Mrs. Peagilly, and that knowledge brought on another torturous wave of self-recrimination. Trinity loathed self-pity, and yet here she stood with Mrs. Peagilly lying on a plank a few feet away, her body wrapped in sailcloth and tied round and round with thick rope, and Trinity fretted about *her* future.

"Amen," everyone chorused.

Shaken from her troublesome reverie, Trinity whispered, "Amen."

Four sailors stepped forward and, with reverence and gentleness she would not have believed them capable of, gently lifted the board upon which Mrs. Peagilly lay in eternal slumber.

Her body slid from the plank—probably a piece of decking—and splashed into the sea two blinks later.

Wincing, Trinity closed her eyes.

With her adventuresome spirit and love of travel, Mrs. Peagilly would've liked a burial at sea. That much Trinity was confident of.

She would have to write Mrs. Peagilly's nephew and tell him the sad news, as well as arrange to return her employer's possessions to England. Most had been shipped ahead and awaited them at a hotel. There were a few larger trunks in the ship's hold as well.

As much as she loathed doing so, Trinity had no choice but to go through Mrs. Peagilly's personal effects to locate the hotel, the translator, and her nephew's address. And money.

It would take money to ship Mrs. Peagilly's belongings back to England.

Except, Mrs. Peagilly had turned the bulk of her funds over to the captain to secure inside the new Chubb safe in his cabin.

A familiar, comforting melody drew her attention.

Devin held a small, oddly-shaped instrument to his lips and played a soulful rendition of *"Amazing Grace."* A sailor strumming a lute joined him, and another raised a violin to his chin as a third put a short wooden flute to his mouth. A fourth man, possessing a version of the same strange wind instrument as Devin, listened for a moment before closing his eyes and harmonizing.

The wind stilled, and the sails eased into slacked folds. Silence and an uncanny peace shrouded the ship as they played on, the water lapping gently at the ship's hull.

When the last note faded, Trinity dabbed at the tears burning her eyes, and Mrs. McKinnick blew her nose.

Georgie slipped his hand into Trinity's, bringing a nascent smile to her lips.

The stoic little fellow, expression somber, said nothing but sucked contentedly on his thumb. He pulled it out, looked at it with maturity and seriousness beyond his four years, then glanced up at Trinity.

"I believe it is time I put this childish habit behind me."

Adorable little man.

She squeezed his other hand.

"That is very grown up of you, Georgie."

He gave a grave nod. "I have attended my fiwst funewal. I am not the child I was yestewday."

Tragic but true.

Trinity was not the optimistic, enthusiastic woman she had been yesterday either.

His mother drew near and hugged Trinity.

"My deepest condolences, Miss Ablethorne. Please let us know if there is anything Sir Godfrey and I can do for you."

Do you need a governess?

Know anyone who might need a companion in Morocco?

Can you loan me funds to return to England?

And do what?

Become a burden to one of her childhood friends until she could find a position?

Instead of blurting the questions, Trinity managed a wan smile. "Thank you."

Trinity had not known Mrs. Peagilly well enough to truly grieve for the woman. Only Devin knew how very brief her employment status had been. She felt like a fake and a fraud for accepting commiserations.

She lifted her focus, her gaze meshing with Devin's.

His all-black, expensively tailored jacket and pantaloons emphasized his athletic physique. In comparison, Misters Meriwether and Truman-Shelton appeared foppish and pallid in their matching pinstripes.

Devin's devastatingly sympathetic smile sent another lump scuttling up her throat and more tears burned behind her eyelids. The wind resumed and played with a lock of dark hair flopped over his forehead.

How old was he?

Not yet thirty, she would guess.

And yet, as the son of a wealthy merchant, he was a partial ship owner and on his way to what might be a grand adventure. Devin could do most anything he chose. His future was secure.

If only that were true for her too.

"Miss Ablethorne, would you join me in my cabin for a glass of sherry and a small repast in Mrs. Peagilly's honor?" Captain Breckett asked.

"That is kind of you, Captain," Trinity said, even as her empty stomach gurgled a complaint, her belly button gnawing at her spine. "And I gratefully accept."

Normally, Trinity did not partake in spirits. She did not like the taste, but she would make an exception today. Besides, she was famished. Other than the few mouthfuls of porridge she choked down yesterday morning, she had not eaten.

Captain Breckett sent his gaze around those gathered nearby. "Mr. Everingham, Mr. Truman-Shelton, Mr. Meriwether, Mr. and Mrs. McKinnick?"

It was gracious of the captain to include everyone. The longer Trinity knew him, the more she admired and respected him.

Mrs. McKinnick shook her head.

"Thank you, Captain, but I shall pass on your generous offer. The children and I shall take a nap. None of us slept well last night."

Word of Mrs. Peagilly's untimely passing had buzzed through the ship in a matter of minutes. No one appeared well-rested other than Mr. Compton.

Facing her husband, Mrs. McKinnick laid a hand on his arm. "But you do go along, dear. Enjoy a toast in memory of dear Mrs. Peagilly."

Her eyes filled with tears again.

Trinity was not sure if the woman's delicate condition contributed to her emotional state or if she wept easily.

"I shan't stay long, darling." He pecked her cheek before she escorted her offspring toward the stairs. "Have a lie-down. I shall ask Cook to prepare a nice tea for you afterward."

Devin approached, still holding the vessel-like

instrument. "May I escort you?"

A scowl marring his handsome features, Mr. Compton halted several feet away.

Had he been of the same inclination as Devin?

She felt his accusing, almost possessive stare boring into her.

Other than the first night, they'd had no more time alone, so why would he think he had a claim on her?

"I am hardly in need of an escort." Trinity's reply was as much for Mr. Compton's benefit as Devin's. Besides, it was true. This was not London.

The second officer canted his head and momentarily disappeared below. That meant Mr. Alderton was the officer in charge. Odd, but she found that reassuring.

Of course, Mr. Compton must be perfectly capable, but his demeanor became more off-putting with each passing day.

The others moved toward the hatchway too.

She pointed to Devin's instrument as he fell in step beside her. "What is that?"

"It is a type of vessel flute. I am unsure of the actual name. I do know, however, that versions date back several hundred years and that similar instruments have been found in many cultures. It was a gift from my father from one of his journeys abroad."

"Very, very old," the sailor possessing a similar unique instrument said, clasping his calloused hands around the flute and bowing. "I am Bandar Amzil. This was my great-grandfather's flute, given to him by a Spaniard many moons ago and passed down from son to son to son."

His coffee brown eyes alight with pleasure, Devin grinned and offered the man his hand.

Trinity had noticed that about him.

He treated everyone equally—with dignity and respect, regardless of their social standing, unlike Mr. Compton.

One would think a man of Devin's wealth would be more arrogant and condescending than a ship's second officer. Unless aristocrats perched somewhere in Mr. Compton's family tree, thus giving him a sense of bloated importance.

Knowing nothing about either man's family, Trinity could only draw upon her observations. Devin was a rogue, a man about town, but he was also kind and considerate. Mr. Compton seemed a polished gentleman, but his behavior suggested he was not as honorable and decent as he portrayed.

What was it Mrs. Shepherd used to say?

Ah, yes.

Do not look on outward appearances, but at the

heart—which, of course, was a paraphrased scripture as was Mrs. Shepherd's habit.

In the case of both men, Trinity did not know either well enough to form an opinion. But an inkling? Yes, that she had already done, right or wrong.

"I heard you playing last night, Mr. Amzil," Devin said. "The melody was lovely but unfamiliar to me."

"Yes, *sahib*," Mr. Amzil said in his lilting voice. "I am Moroccan. I play the music of my ancestors."

"I should like to play together again." Devin tipped his mouth into a genuine smile. "I am Devin Everingham, and this is Miss Trinity Ablethorne."

"It would be my pleasure." Mr. Amzil turned those black eyes on Trinity. "I play for the lady too."

"I would be honored." Though the day was not cold, a vulnerability Trinity had never experienced assailed her, and she wrapped her cloak tighter around her. She had not realized how much she depended on Mrs. Peagilly's wealth of knowledge.

"We should go below," Devin said. "The captain is waiting. I look forward to speaking with you further, Mr. Amzil. I could use a bit of instruction and advice about Morocco. I have a business enterprise here that may require an extended stay."

"It would be my greatest pleasure." Another smile encompassed the Moroccan's face. "I am returning home after an eight-year absence. This is my last voyage. I have missed my homeland for too long." He held his hands to his chest. "I am at your disposal now and after the ship docks."

If only Trinity were as fortunate.

She did not even know the name of the interpreter Mrs. Peagilly was to have met in Casablanca.

Devin nodded, looking well pleased and perhaps a tinge relieved as well. "I would value a man of your knowledge and expertise aiding me. We can discuss the details later if you are interested in a position."

"It is no accident that our paths crossed, sahib." Mr. Amzil tucked his flute into a hidden pocket inside his long shirt. "I am amendable to the idea."

"Excellent." Devin touched her arm. "We should go."

"All will be well, miss." Mr. Amzil flashed a broad smile, his square teeth a bright contrast to his dark skin. He said it with such confidence and assurance she could almost believe him.

Without funds or friends, Trinity had a mere day, mayhap two, to figure out what she would do when they reached the Port of Casablanca.

9

Sir, I pray this letter finds you in a timely manner. I know you wished to remain abroad for an undetermined while, but your mother has fallen gravely ill with diphtheria.

Three of the servants, including your mother's personal maid, are also infected, leading the physician to surmise one of them contracted the disease and spread it to the others. The household is in quarantine and unable to move to Essex.

I have spoken with the physician, and I am sorry to say, he is not optimistic about Mrs. Everingham's recovery, as complications have already set in. In truth, he asked how speedily you might return to England, hence, this unsolicited and presumptuous letter.

I await your response and directives. Meanwhile, under difficult and unforeseen circumstances, I presume you wish me to pay the physician's fees and the expenses necessary for the household's continued presence in London.

~Mr. Milton Shillingford, in an urgent letter to
Mr. Devin Everingham
Posted via the *Relentless Righteousness* en route to
Casablanca five days after Devin's departure

Outside Trinity's stateroom
That same evening

Hand raised to rap on Trinity's quarters, Devin hesitated. All day, he'd sought a chance to speak with her privately, but none had arisen. He also did not want to be an insensitive clodpate, understanding she needed time to overcome her grief and her reduced circumstances.

Though she had not said as much, her expressive eyes betrayed her fear, vulnerability, and uncertainty.

He had no choice but to assist her.

Duchess, the ship's resident vermin catcher, chirped as she approached, tail high. She circled Devin's legs before giving a soft meow and padding away, no doubt for her evening hunt.

A sailor's mournful tune sifted below deck as the *Daunting Duchess* creaked and groaned in an endless chorus of vessel, water, and waves.

Earlier today, Devin had approached Sir Godfrey on Trinity's behalf, without her knowledge, and inquired if he and his wife might need a governess. Georgie and Gladys had taken to Trinity, and she to them.

Unfortunately, the McKinnicks did not need a governess.

As part of Sir Godfrey's diplomatic assignment, provisions had been arranged for a governess, tutor, and nurse for his children. In fact, he had explained, the household staff and all other help he might require awaited his family's arrival—all prearranged by the British government.

If Sir Godfrey found any of the servants unsatisfactory, he could replace them. However, to show his trust, support, and admiration for the Moroccan people, he believed it wise and improved relationships by employing qualified locals rather than inserting English staff.

Devin could not argue against his logic, but it also seemed unwise to rely totally upon people one did not know, particularly as a stranger in a foreign land. Only, Sir Godfrey was not relying entirely on the benevolence of the Moroccans. An armed contingent of British soldiers would meet the McKinnicks at the harbor, escort them to their home, and remain at the vast walled estate to provide ongoing security.

Sir Godfrey did offer to ask around and see if any other foreign consuls needed a companion or governess. That would take time, however, and Devin would leave for Fez three days after the *Daunting Duchess* made port *if* everything Mr. Shillingford had prearranged was in order.

Otherwise…

Devin did not want to contemplate that inconvenience. Nonetheless, he would manage.

If his father could travel the world and become proficient at it, then by God above, he would too. Father had not had to deal with a tempting female who, through no fault of hers, found herself stranded in a land not always hospitable to European women.

An unescorted, attractive young woman like Trinity would face certain danger.

That knowledge left a sour taste in his mouth.

Devin could not desert her.

She was not his responsibility, but he had voluntarily taken on that burden until she made other arrangements.

No one else would.

Mr. Compton's features swam across his mind, and Devin scowled.

Would Thaddeus Compton?

How?

Short of marrying Trinity so she could remain aboard the ship until the *Daunting Duchess* returned to England, what could Compton do? That was *if* the captain approved of the match. An officer with a wife on board led to all sorts of sticky situations.

Jealousy, swift and acrid, twisted a sharp, serrated blade in Devin's belly.

That blighter did not deserve her.

Besides, didn't officers share quarters?

Stop. Your imagination borders on lunacy.

Besides, nothing in Trinity's interactions with Compton suggested a romantic inclination on her part.

But what about his?

More than once, Compton had behaved like a jealous suitor.

Devin booted the aggravating thought aside.

On a happier note, his conversation with Bandar Amzil had gone extremely well. Tired of life at sea and missing his homeland and family, the middling-aged man was happy to accept a position as an interpreter, guide, man of business, and any other capacity Devin might need him.

Devin preferred to work with someone he knew rather than rely exclusively on the strangers Shillingford had hired, though many of them would still be necessary. Regardless, that still left the issue of what to do with Trinity.

Bandar also expressed concern for her. "The port and the city are not safe for pretty, young, unmarried European women," he said, concern pleating his face and crinkling the corners of his eyes. "Not safe at all. There are evil men with eyes everywhere."

His black-eyed gaze had shifted, veering toward Meriwether and Truman-Shelton.

Had he also deduced those seemingly unremarkable

men were not what they presented?

In truth, Trinity might not be amendable to Devin's help but instead see his offer as interference or, worse yet, machinations. He, above all people, understood how irritating and frustrating it was to have someone else take it upon themselves to control one's life and steer it in a direction one neither wanted nor expected to go.

For instance, marriage to an empty-headed ninny who could not tell time. Pitiful, malleable Miss Marsters-Montgomery. Pray to God her grandmother had intervened on the girl's behalf.

Sighing, Devin thinned his mouth into a taut line before giving a single soft rap upon Trinity's door. It could not be comfortable for her to remain in the cabin where Mrs. Peagilly died.

He could offer to exchange quarters with her, but she was fiercely independent and would likely refuse. He admired her gumption—her spirit and pluck. Regardless, there was no shame in accepting help.

He had the impression she had relied upon herself most, if not all, of her life.

Since his conversation with Captain Breckett last night, Devin had gone round and round with possible solutions to Trinity's troublesome situation. The most obvious and easiest remedy was to pay for passage back to England.

However, there was the matter of locating a ship with an available berth. Often, passages were booked months in advance.

He supposed it was too much to hope that a suitable vessel was docked at Casablanca and shortly after the *Daunting Duchess* made port would sail. Not just any passenger-carrying vessel would do either. Many unscrupulous scoundrels just this side of pirates manned sailing ships offering passenger accommodations— filthy, rat-infested common quarters that made Devin's humble cabin on the *Daunting Duchess* seem a bedchamber at Buckingham Palace.

If Trinity had to wait to sail, which was likely the case, what would Devin do with her in the meanwhile? He'd had almost suggested that Trinity reside with the McKinnicks until she sailed back to England, but then he discovered they were not staying in Casablanca.

Better for her to remain near the harbor, in any event. There she stood a greater chance of booking an immediate passage if a cabin became available. However, as with most port cities, the docks and piers were among the most dangerous areas, and he did not know where else she could stay.

Which brought him back to square one.

What was he to do with her in the meantime?

In truth, he did not relish the idea of her sailing home alone either.

Nevertheless, he could not remain in Casablanca for weeks waiting on a ship for her. Besides, even this far from England, it would not be respectable for them to have rooms in the same hotel. Unchaperoned as she was, no one would believe that midnight assignations weren't commonplace.

Captain Breckett had strongly warned against her going anywhere or being left anywhere by herself, and that included a hotel room. Evidently, Mrs. Peagilly, an experienced traveler, had prearranged an entire entourage for her venture well in advance, including armed guards.

Then there was the issue of the sickness the captain had mentioned.

What sort of sickness, and how widespread was it?

Forefinger knuckle bent, Devin knocked again, this time a trifle louder.

"Trinity? It is Devin," he said, mindful to keep his voice low.

His checking on her was not improper, but he would rather not alert the other passengers.

If the winds continued, the captain estimated they'd make port the day after tomorrow in the afternoon. That left blasted scarce time to make arrangements for her.

Devin had just lifted his hand to knock again when the latch squeaked, and the door creaked open.

Trinity's rich chestnut hair hung over her shoulders and down to her trim waist. She had resumed wearing the slate gray gown, likely because it was the closest thing to mourning black she owned. It stripped the color from her alabaster skin and turned her eyes indigo.

Her face sleep-softened, Trinity blinked drowsily at him.

She looked utterly done in. And adorable.

He wanted to take her into his arms, kiss the crown of her head and that delectable dimple in her chin, and assure her everything would be fine. Except, he could not because it would not. Even if Bandar had proclaimed that it would.

"I am sorry, Devin. I fell asleep and did not hear you knocking."

Remorse tunneled through his blood for waking her.

She had used his given name again, whether due to exhaustion lowering her defenses or because she'd become familiar enough with him these past days that she did not think it necessary to uphold strictures.

Poor darling.

She needed to rest. The purplish circles beneath her eyes earlier today and her current pallor were an indisputable testament to that.

"I am sorry I woke you, Trinity, but we should

make Casablanca the day after tomorrow, and I wanted to discuss your plans."

Shock flitted across her pale face, and she clasped her hands together before she schooled her features into a benign mien.

"That soon?" Glancing over her shoulder, she murmured. "I intended to go through Mrs. Peagilly's effects to discover her plans for our arrival. I thought that might help me decide the best course of action."

A good plan.

She tugged the corner of her lower lip into her mouth. "I am not sure that is entirely ethical, and it makes me feel intrusive and like a criminal, but I do not have a choice."

"No, you do not." Had she eaten dinner? She had barely touched the fare Captain Breckett had prepared after the funeral, though she'd filled her plate. "Would you like help?"

She shot him an astonished glance.

"I would, in truth. I started to, but as I said, I fell asleep."

If Mrs. Peagilly had paid in advance for a hotel or other lodgings, as well as the other services she had arranged, then a refund was due, but that was not Trinity's responsibility. Mayhap Bandar could see to those details on her behalf.

"Let's get to it, shall we?" he suggested.

Assisting Trinity would provide an opportunity to discuss her plans.

Pale and drawn, she appeared fragile and ready to collapse.

That protective instinct swelled within him again.

Devin would not leave her.

He could not, which put him in a deuced difficult situation, blast his eyes.

"Yes, of course." She stepped aside, and he brushed past her, inhaling her subtle scent.

Spring flowers and a hint of Castile soap, if he was not mistaken.

After a moment's hesitation, she softly closed the door.

Probably for the best. Even though this was necessary, others might take exception.

And then there were those two swindlers who might try to take advantage of the tragedy. So far, there had been no further talk of an investment with Devin. Interestingly, he'd come upon them in deep conversation with Mr. Compton in the saloon and on deck.

The second mate did not seem the gullible sort, but mayhap Devin should warn him. Except that any advice he tried to give Compton would be as welcome as a viper bite. Still, Devin could not stay silent and see Compton conned.

"There is a satchel on the desk." Trinity pointed to the floral tapestry bag beside a short pile of papers. Her cabin was nearly identical to his, except hers was located on the ship's port side rather than the starboard.

"You could start there," she said. "I shall go through her trunk. I am not sure what I am looking for, though."

"All right." Devin rubbed an eyebrow. "Letters, receipts, anything that would indicate who she expected to meet or where she planned on staying."

After shoving her hair over her shoulders, she placed her hands on her hips. "She has more luggage and crates in the cargo hold."

Yet Trinity only had one small trunk.

"Captain Breckett is holding her valuables in his safe, but I assume she would have kept necessary and important papers with her." Her voice caught, and she swallowed, the slender column of her throat working as she struggled for control.

The darling tried so hard to be brave.

"I ought to have asked her about the details, but I did not want to seem forward or intrusive." Self-castigation and chagrin thickened her voice. Or mayhap tears caused the huskiness.

On impulse, Devin turned around and gathered her into his embrace.

At first, Trinity stiffened. Then, with a sigh, she sagged into Devin, burying her face in his chest and wrapping her arms around his waist as she wept softly.

"There's a love," he murmured into that mass of silken curls. "You will come through this. I promise. I shall help you."

10

Ronan says news of a plague outbreak has reached the harbormaster. Two ships, newly arrived from West Africa, are under quarantine. I cannot help but fret for Trinity, for the harbors of Tangiers and Casablanca may soon be closed to prevent the further spread of the contagion. I pray our friend is well and safe.

~Mrs. Mercy Brockman,
in a letter to Mrs. Faith Kellinggrave

Still in Trinity's stateroom

Sniffling, Trinity nodded, too mortified to meet Devin's sympathetic gaze. She had not meant to dissolve into tears. His compassion had breached her fortifications, and the dratted tears had spilled from her eyes, despite her forbidding them to flow.

Come now, Trinity Samantha Honoria Shepard Ablethorne. You are made of sterner stuff. You are strong. Independent. Capable. Resilient.

True, but at this moment, she merely needed someone to hold her. Someone to be strong for her. For so long, she'd relied only on herself, and the truth was that it was wonderful to depend on someone else, if only for a few minutes.

Honestly, she could not recall the last time anyone had hugged her, other than a brief embrace by one of her girlhood friends. In this tiny cabin on a ship sailing across the Atlantic Ocean, without friends or family, uncertain what the future held for her, and utterly at the mercy of Fate's fickleness, she could not summon her usual stoicism and fortitude.

Not that Trinity truly believed in fate or luck. As a woman of strong faith, she had always believed in the power of prayer and God's destiny and purpose. Still, even the most devoted person was allowed a moment of weakness.

Weren't they?

"We shall think of something," Devin said. "It is not as bad as all of that."

It was, and he knew it.

Nevertheless, Trinity's heart softened a fraction more at his attempt to comfort her.

She welcomed his arms encircling her in a tender yet strong embrace—savored the succor that laying her face against the wide expanse of his chest offered. And, yes, she admitted secretly to herself, she delighted in the soft kisses he pressed to her scalp while murmuring soothing words and nonsensical promises.

He smelled of shaving lotion, soap, and the merest hint of sea air.

Devin Everingham might be a rogue, a deucedly tempting one, but he was also kind.

Trinity had misjudged him.

Last night, after Mrs. Peagilly's body had been removed, Trinity had lain in the upper bunk, staring at the ceiling. She'd gone over and over every scenario, attempting to find a solution to her quandary.

Mrs. Peagilly had not minced words about the possible perils when she had offered Trinity employment. Just two days ago, she had reiterated the dangers.

"You must never, and I do mean *never*, Trinity, venture anywhere alone. I have hired several guards to protect us. They will meet us at the ship. You would not be the first young European woman to go missing if you do not heed my advice. Women are sold as sex slaves all over Africa, and blue-eyed women are in particular demand."

A shiver scuttled up Trinity's spine.

She might be able to borrow funds for passage, but she had no means to repay them until she found a new position or a place to stay until a ship was available to take her home.

In his quarters earlier—in an awkward and disconcerting conversation—Captain Breckett politely denied her request to remain on the *Daunting Duchess*.

All the cabins were promised to passengers leaving Morocco

Trinity had been eager to leave her last post because it was boring. More fool her. She would take boring now if it meant security.

Would she really?

Bah, when had she become fickle and flighty? Doubleminded?

At least she could stop feeling sorry for herself, for pity's sake.

Inhaling a ragged breath, she lifted her head, her face averted to hide her red-rimmed eyes.

"I apologize." She retreated a step and swiped at her face, catching sight of the dark stain on Devin's fine Kersey wool coat. "I have dampened your coat front."

With a sideways grin hitching his mouth up on one side, he lifted her chin. "It is just a coat. It will dry." *And likely stain.* "You are more important."

Shaking her head, she furrowed her forehead. "How can you say that when you barely know me?"

"I know you better than you think."

"Oh?" Arms crossed, she raised a skeptical eyebrow. "What do you know about me?"

"You are unselfish and conscientious. You are an orphan and have no family. You are kind, gentle, patient, helpful, and generous."

She rolled her eyes. "You make me sound like a saint, which I assure you, I am not."

He disregarded her sarcasm and continued to list her qualities. "You are educated, sketch admirably, dislike spirits, and possess common sense, excellent manners, and admirable decorum."

"Are you positive?" she quipped, feeling much more lighthearted than she had five minutes ago, which no doubt was his intent.

The sly, disarming bounder.

"Oh, indeed," he said with mock severity.

She snorted.

Chuckling, Devin winked at her unladylike behavior.

"You are fond of licorice and lemon drops, your perfume is light and refreshing like a spring morning, and you also study the stars."

"You heard that?" So enraptured had Trinity been peering through Mr. Compton's night telescope that she had not noticed Devin that first night.

"I did."

This man... Trinity could grow to care for him. Perhaps she had already begun to.

Which was the epitome of imprudence.

He was a rogue. A rake. A scoundrel.

She had seen him in action first hand.

And yet…

That Devin remembered all those insignificant details about her caused an unnameable emotion to bloom behind her breastbone and take root in her heart. A powerful sentiment that brought a new surge of moisture to her eyes but one not induced by grief, fear, or pain.

In point of fact, Trinity was not positive she could list as many attributes about Devin.

His gaze darkened, the empathy and kindness fading from the brown orbs as something much more thrilling replaced the emotions. He cupped Trinity's chin, his eyes holding hers captive, the spark of desire in those smoldering pools growing into a mesmerizing magnetism she could not look away from—did not want to look away from.

His focus dipped to her parted mouth.

"Trinity."

He breathed her name with such reverence and awe that her toes curled in her half-boots.

"Sweet, lovely Trinity."

Her pulse fluttered and quickened into double time.

What was this madness?

She should tell him to go. To stop wooing her with seductive words and scorching glances. But not only could she not, but she also did not want to.

Heavens no.

She must explore whatever this was burgeoning between them.

He beckoned to her silently, relentlessly, and she was powerless to stop herself from raising her face and offering her mouth.

Then Devin's lips were upon hers. Hot and firm and delicious and heady.

Oh, so heady.

She gripped his muscled biceps to keep from sagging into a molten puddle on the rough floor.

His kiss grew more intense, more demanding, as he crushed her to his chest.

Yes. Yes.

A primal groan escaped him as he grazed his mouth over Trinity's cheeks, jaw, and neck. All the while, he boldly caressed her back and shoulders, invoking sensations she'd never experienced before.

Head thrown back, she allowed him access to her throat, her mind a dizzy haze, unable to think. All she could do was feel.

Devin's heat. His caresses. His blistering kisses.

"Sweet Trinity," he murmured again before taking her mouth once more in a soul-shattering kiss.

He plundered the depths of her mouth, and rather than be shocked or pull away—oh, no indeed—Trinity pressed even closer. Needing to feel Devin. To smell him. To taste him.

His breathing coming in ragged gasps, he set her away from him, almost roughly.

Lost, bereft, she reached for him.

"If I continue, sweeting, I shan't be able to stop."

"Oh." Dazed, her lips swollen and her blood singing, Trinity put two fingers to her mouth.

She had never been kissed before, let alone by an experienced rake.

Shouldn't she be ashamed?

Shocked?

Of something so glorious? So blissful? So right?

No. No.

Furthermore, she would not deny her culpability. She'd kissed Devin back and would not throw silly, theatrical accusations at him now. However, she must gather her scattered wits and consider her reputation.

"I think you should go, Devin. Before we make a monumental mistake."

Before she begged him to stay, reputation, common sense, and propriety be hanged.

Despite the chaos raging inside, only the merest tremor afflicted her voice.

Eyes hooded, he regarded her for a long, tense moment. So long, in fact, that her already taut nerves stretched nearly to the point of shattering.

"Trinity?"

Trinity could not prevent the tiny, pleased smile from tipping her lips upward. She adored it when Devin said her name, his tenor deep and husky. As if he was caught up in the same tidal wave of emotion and desire.

"Yes?"

The sultry voice did not sound like her, but rather a wanton's—a woman of the world offering a wicked invitation. That would never do, even if it were partially true.

She cleared her throat. "Yes?"

A trifle better, but not as unruffled and composed as she would've liked.

"I think I have stumbled upon the perfect solution to your being stranded in Casablanca. It is a answer to a long-standing dilemma for me as well. I believe it would benefit us both. Honestly, I do not see a disadvantage and do not know why I did not think of it earlier."

He continued to look at her like she was a pastry he could barely refrain from gobbling up.

How could something be simultaneously thrilling and unsettling?

A tiny spark of hope sprang to life, nonetheless.

"You have?"

Mayhap he had a position to offer her. Faith Kellinggrave had been Lord Constantine's scrivener before they married. Except, Trinity was not trained as a scribe.

A secretary?

She supposed she could manage those duties, and she was a quick learner.

Devin nodded, then raked his fingers through his thick hair, the movement telling. He was not as confident of his solution as he pretended.

He cleared his throat.

Yes, most definitely apprehensive.

Probably not an offer of employment, then.

At least—not a respectable one.

Pain and disappointment deluged her, squeezing her lungs and heart in an unmerciful, vice-like grip.

God rot the bounder for giving Trinity hope and then dashing it into a thousand pieces with no more care than discarding an empty whisky bottle.

Taking her palms in his, Devin ran his thumbs over the backs of her hands.

Even knowing what he was about to suggest, a thrill spiraled up her arms and spread across her shoulders. He had merely to touch her, and she became pliable clay in his strong hands.

You are a fool, Trinity. A silly, stupid, gullible fool.

Oh, Devin Everingham was a skilled seducer. She would give him that.

However, he'd soon discover that Trinity was not easily beguiled.

"Trinity, I have a proposition."

The miniscule hope that she had misunderstood his intention, that she had been wrong, dissolved. Pain, disbelief, and offense tangled into a confused, angry knot in her stomach, and she wanted to slap the confident expression from his handsome face.

Except, she had never hit anyone in her entire life, even if planting him a facer at this moment would give her tremendous satisfaction.

"I shan't be your mistress," she snapped, snatching her hands away.

To be used, degraded, and eventually tossed aside when someone more intriguing and tantalizing came along. Never.

"Pardon?" Devin jerked as if slapped.

Anger flashed in the depths of his chocolatey eyes, and for half a second, Trinity feared his reaction. The ire eased from his expression, and tenderness replaced his wrath.

"I would never presume to insult you with such a vulgar suggestion." He lifted her hand to his mouth and brushed his lips across the knuckles.

Trinity's traitorous knees trembled, and her heart skipped a beat before resuming an irregular tempo.

Foolish, foolish girl.

"I want you to marry me, sweeting."

11

Forgive me, son. I wish you were here for me to ask for your forgiveness in person. I fear I may not live until I see you again, and I have many, so very many regrets. I drove you from me, just as I did your father.

My pride has been my greatest flaw, followed closely by criticism and discontent. I could've lived a happy, blessed life; instead, I ruined all I had been given because I coveted more prestige.

And in the end, what does it matter whether one is nobly born or a pauper? It is how one lived one's life, the good one accomplished, and the legacy one leaves behind. I have failed miserably in that respect, except for you. You are the one thing I am proud of.

You are a good, decent man like your father was.

I do love you, Devin. I did not show you or tell you as I should have done, which is my biggest regret. That and I shall never see what an exceptional father I know you shall be.

~Mrs. Desdemona Everingham, to her son, Devin
Dictated to her physician—never posted

Still in Trinity's cabin
Ten perfectly silent and tension-filled seconds later

Trinity opened and closed her mouth thrice, but no sound emerged.

Devin could not prevent the chuckle that escaped him.

He had successfully rendered her speechless.

"Pardon?" she whispered.

"I said, I want to marry you. Before we dock, Captain Breckett can perform the ceremony."

"I heard you." She gaped at him. "I just cannot believe what I heard."

She eyed him as one might a lunatic.

Mayhap he was mad.

It was a madcap idea.

"You cannot be serious, Devin. We've known each other for less than a week. Besides, Captain Breckett cannot legally marry us."

Actually, four days if he did not count their first meeting at the Mumfords' house party, for which, for all accounts and purposes, she'd been invisible to him.

The ship pitched, and she braced herself with a hand on the upper bunk.

Perchance her affections lay elsewhere.

Blast. Devin had not considered that possibility.

He cocked his head. "Is there someone who holds your heart?"

"No." She shook her head, causing the lush curls to sway. "But that doesn't mean I shall marry you. What do you take me for?"

Such relief engulfed him that he nearly grinned. However, given Trinity still looked at him like he had either grown horns or was dicked in the nob—perhaps both—he checked his jubilation.

"An extremely desirable, intelligent woman I would be honored to make my wife."

In truth, no other lady had ever tempted Devin—a self-proclaimed, on-the-road-to-redemption rogue—to propose matrimony. From the moment his eyes had met hers that first night, something had sparked between them, whether she recognized the attraction or not.

Eyes narrowed, Trinity pointed at him, her demeanor shouting suspicion and a little bewilderment too.

She thought he jested.

Her doubt fairly radiated off her.

"Pray tell me, Devin, how our exchanging vows solves a problem for you."

Devin probably shouldn't have mentioned that detail during his wholly unromantic proposal. But if this woman were to be his wife, then there would be no secrets between them.

Cupping his nape, he thinned his mouth into a tense ribbon and scuffed a boot on the floor. Even now, halfway across the ocean, Mother's meddling raised his ire.

"My mother is determined that I should marry into the aristocracy. She has become fanatical and possibly unhinged in her pursuit of that goal. Her grandfather, my great-grandfather, was an earl. She did everything in her power, including convincing a young woman to crawl into my bed in the wee morning hours at a house party, to entrap me into marriage. Thank God, the chit mistook a matron's room for mine."

Trinity gasped and pressed a fine-boned hand to her chest. "She did not."

"She did." Devin arched an eyebrow. "I shall leave you to imagine the scene when Lady Hornbellow awoke."

"Good Lord." Rather than outrage or disbelief, mirth sparkled in Trinity's blue eyes, and she covered her mouth. Nonetheless, a giggle escaped.

"Was it?" She swallowed another chuckle. "Was it very dreadful?"

"Extremely." Devin grimaced, his mouth turned down in distaste. "The poor girl, who hasn't the sense of a potato, did not even think to lie. She admitted she had thought the room was mine, but she'd always confused her right from her left and accidentally mixed up the rooms."

"Oh, dear." To her credit, Trinity did not laugh again, but her mouth twitched, and jollity danced in her eyes. "Probably not an ideal candidate for a wife for you, I agree."

"Exactly." Devin snorted. "Plus, if she is a month beyond her sixteenth birthday, I shall eat my gloves."

"You still have not explained how our union would solve your dilemma." It seemed tenacity was another admirable quality Trinity possessed.

"I am on this ship due to my mother's interference. I am convinced she will stop at nothing to see me leg-shackled to a blueblood, which by the way, I have no interest in doing. Ever. My father has—had—business ventures all over the world. I decided it was past time for me to take an interest in his enterprises personally."

"And?" She tapped her toe.

He was rambling.

Get to it, Devin Wesley Rayburn Everingham.

"In short, if I take you to wife—a woman of my choosing whom I admire and respect—Mother will have to cease and desist."

"You would marry someone you barely know to spite your mother?"

"No, not to spite her. To spare me entrapment in a marriage to a woman I might not be able to stand." He gave her a devilish wink and a sideways smile. "I can *more* than stand you."

He dropped his focus to her cherry-red lips.

Very much more.

Her cheeks glowed pink at his meaning.

"I barely know you, Devin."

"What do you want to know?"

She stared at him mutely, then gave a rueful shrug and shook her head. "I do not even know how old you are."

"My full name is Devin Wesley Rayburn Everingham. I am six and twenty. My birthday is March third. My favorite color is red. I like dogs and cats, but not big birds." He scratched his chin. "A hawk attacked me as a child, and raptors have given me the shivers ever since."

That caused a tiny smile, more disbelief than true humor.

"I can never have enough plum pudding or crumpets with butter and preserves but cannot abide custard, head cheese, or pickled eggs. I enjoy orchestras but not vocalists as much. I ride, fence, swim, dance, and play the ocarina and pianoforte. I like children, would like to own a parrot someday, and I do not employ a valet."

Giving a flourishing bow, he grinned. "Now, you now know the most important things about me."

"You are ridiculous."

He drew near and placed his hands on her shoulders.

"And you are the only woman I have ever considered marrying. I sincerely believe we would do well together, Trinity."

"A marriage of convenience?" She puzzled her brow, a hint of sadness in her eyes. "Is that what you are suggesting?"

"I hope we can make it something more, even if that is how it begins." No sense in pretending he was madly in love with her. Devin desired her. She intrigued him, but love was not part of the equation.

Her expression inscrutable, she gazed past him. "I never thought to marry, so you will understand why the notion of a marriage of convenience never crossed my mind."

"I know it is not ideal, but by marrying me, you are assured safety in Morocco. You can travel with me if you like, or if you prefer, you can stay at one of my houses in England."

She gave him a side-eyed glance, skepticism radiating from her. "You have more than one house?"

"Yes." He nodded. "Four, in point of fact. Although my mother is currently in residence at the Essex estate."

Putting a hand to her forehead, she drew in a long breath. "It is such a permanent solution to a temporary problem. One, I cannot help but think, that we would come to regret."

"There are no guarantees in life." Devin shrugged and widened his stance as the ship pitched again, this time more violently.

"In truth, Trinity, I think arranged marriages have advantages. There are no false expectations. No misunderstandings. No misplaced hopes and dreams. Fewer disappointments. If the union turns out better than anticipated, that is a blessing."

His parents had married for love, but that had not assured their happiness.

Clasping her hands, she studied his features.

"What if we discover we cannot abide one another, Devin? Annulments are nearly impossible to attain. You would be shackled to me, and I with you, for the rest of our lives."

She raised a shoulder. "That bears consideration. A whim, or whatever this is, probably is not the wisest course."

"It is a risk I am willing to take. With you, Trinity. Only you."

He drew near and touched her petal-soft cheek, then kissed her forehead. He *wanted* to take care of her, to take her as his wife.

Like a coward, he had fled England believing wedlock was not in his near future, and here he was, trying to persuade this most remarkable of women to accept his suit.

"If the day comes and you want to leave, Trinity, I shall not stop you. I would provide you with a generous allowance. You shall never want for anything."

Did he hear himself?

He sounded like a man in love.

Which, of course, was ludicrous.

"The risk is greater for me." Wariness colored every word. "You could choose to put me aside."

Was she considering his proposal?

"I shall write a contract with terms you specify and have Captain Breckett, Mr. Alderton, and Sir Godfrey act as witnesses."

She wrinkled her nose. "I do not relish others knowing my business."

"The terms would remain private. They would only assign their signatures to the last page."

"May I have until morning to think about it?"

Her blue-eyed gaze, wide and uncertain, searched his face. "It is a huge, life-altering decision." She bit her lower lip. "I wish we had more time. Marriage is not something to be rushed into."

"I know." Devin kissed her forehead again. "Let me check with Captain Breckett. The wedding must take place in international waters for him to have jurisdiction to perform the ceremony."

It might be too late already, and then what would they do?

Marry in Casablanca?

"I shall speak with him now and return as soon as possible." He scanned his gaze over Mrs. Peagilly's satchel. "Unless you wish me to stay and help go through Mrs. Peagilly's papers."

"No, go." Trinity fashioned a nascent smile. "I need time alone, please."

12

It would be most unwise to visit Fez el-Bali and the Souq—leather bazaar at this time. The plague has reached our borders and has spread throughout the region. Your health would be in jeopardy as many have fallen ill and died. I urge you to reconsider and postpone your inspection until a safer time. I await your response.

~Mr. Jalil Dhabi, overseer of the Chouara Tannery,
in a brief note to Mr. Devin Everingham
delivered to the *Daunting Duchess*
a mere hour after she arrived in port

Trinity's cabin
An hour later

*M*arriage. To Devin.
Trinity shook her head for at least the hundredth time since Devin had left.

She shouldn't be considering his preposterous, imprudent proposal.

She shouldn't.

It was crazy. Impractical. Risky. Impetuous.

Everything she was not.

And yet self-preservation proved a powerful incentive.

Rather than diving straight into Mrs. Peagilly's satchel after his departure, Trinity bathed, cleansed her teeth, and brushed her hair until it snapped and crackled before securing it in a simple chignon.

All that amid the ship's increased pitching and gyrating.

They must've sailed into quite a powerful gale.

Opting to don her navy-blue gown rather than her night rail, she now sat on the hard, uncomfortable chair. With a shawl draped across her shoulders against the unexpected chill, she rested her chin in her hand and glumly stared at Mrs. Peagilly's tapestry bag.

So far, none of the removed contents revealed any life-altering or useful information.

Useful to Trinity, that was.

What a conundrum.

Exchange vows with Devin before the ship reached Morocco, thereby assuring herself provision and safety but relinquishing her freedom for a lifetime to a man she barely knew. Or gambling that something remaining in Mrs. Peagilly's bag contained a miraculous answer to Trinity's problem.

Not a wagerer, Trinity did not like the odds of either option.

The ship lurched, and she cocked her head, listening.

The seas had roughened to such a degree this past hour that she had bumped her head and hip, staggering around the small space.

Mayhap that is why Devin had not returned.

He had taken ill again.

Should she check on him?

He *was* nearly her betrothed.

She certainly was not a giddy, sentimental bride-to-be.

Curling her mouth into a half-grimace, half-sardonic smile, Trinity shook her head.

Circumstances might force her to marry Devin Everingham, but her heart would remain hers if she did. That way, when he grew bored of her, realized he'd made a monumental mistake, or his eye roved, she would not be crushed or devastated.

She would approach the union with reason and clarity, as one entering a mutually beneficial business arrangement would. No feminine histrionics or tears. She was not the first female to make the best of a bad situation, nor would she be the last.

The ship dipped violently again, and Trinity slapped a hand atop the papers to keep them from skidding off the makeshift table and onto the floor.

The captain had not breathed a word about an impending storm earlier. An experienced seaman would not be caught unaware. Had he not wanted to upset the passengers or thought to outrun the weather? Or, had this tempest, indeed, come upon the ship with such swiftness and stealth that he had been unprepared?

Not one to panic or give herself over to unhealthy and unproductive fears, Trinity, nevertheless, could not stifle the stirrings of unease. Still, there was no sense dwelling on the storm. She had a task to finish, not that she truly expected that anything in Mrs. Peagilly's bag would make a difference one way or the other.

After wrapping the shawl tighter around her, she glanced at the door.

Stop it, goose.

He is not coming.

With a determined shake of her head, Trinity turned her attention back to inspecting the contents of Mrs. Peagilly's bag.

So far, Trinity had found a hotel receipt—Riad Les Zarabel—from a man named Zarif Yassine, a few correspondences from Mr. Omar Salmi—the man making the arrangements for the sojourn—a small leather purse containing a few coins, a blue leather-bound journal with EU stamped in gold, and Mrs. Peagilly's itinerary.

They were to have gone to Greece next.

A weak half-smile swept Trinity's mouth upward.

They would've had a grand time. Of that, she had no doubt.

Sighing, she fished out the last papers: a map, more correspondences, a bank receipt for a substantial sum, an address list, and...

Trinity gasped as she finished unfolding the final document.

Mrs. Peagilly's Last Will and Testament, along with a letter from her London solicitor and a letter to her nephew, Vicar Wilfred Howard.

So, Mrs. Peagilly had considered that she might die on this journey.

Why, for heaven's sake, hadn't she said anything to Trinity?

A wave of anger stronger than the winds battering the ship buffeted her but receded after a couple of seconds. As reason surfaced, her irritation melted away as swiftly as snow on a hearth.

In the short time Trinity had known her employer, she had learned the woman was thorough, efficient, and organized. She had likely traveled with a copy of her will since becoming widowed three and forty years ago.

There wasn't so much as a note for Trinity.

Unfortunate but not a surprise.

She eyed the journal.

No. Trinity would not read it.

To do so pushed the bounds—it was too invasive.

Folding her hands and closing her eyes, Trinity bowed her head.

Lord, I need your guidance.

What should I do?

Trust that you will provide for me?

Is Devin's proposal the answer?

She had not agreed to marry Devin—only said she'd think about it.

Heaving a rather hefty, unhappy sigh, Trinity opened her eyes.

No great epiphany had struck her—no clear direction.

After replacing everything in Mrs. Peagilly's bag, Trinity eyed her cloak.

It must be close to midnight, and Devin had not returned. Given the storm caused the ship to sway and heave like an apple in a tub of water, he had probably sought his cabin. In any event, the nuptials could not occur in the middle of the night during a squall.

That gave Trinity more time to decide.

Decide?

What choice did she have?

Only one.

The rapid, triple knock jolted her from her reverie.

"Trinity? Are you awake?"

Devin.

Jumping up so swiftly that the chair almost toppled, she hurried to open the door.

Hair rain slickened, his coat drenched, Devin stood there, paler than he had been an hour ago. No doubt, the effects of the gale howling outside.

He did not mince words but went straight to the point.

"Captain said we must marry tonight while we are still in international waters. I am sorry." Contriteness and sympathy softened his contoured features.

Tonight?

"I see."

"I know you wanted more time, Trinity."

There had only been one choice all along. Part of her—the part she rarely let show—

silently screamed in rebellion at being compelled to marry under these ill-fated circumstances.

"The storm is worsening." Devin pointed his gaze upward. "Captain Breckett said he can only spare five minutes to perform the ceremony."

"When?"

"Now."

Now? *Now?*

Trinity shut her eyes and grasped the doorway.

Another roll of the ship had her eyes flying open.

She had never been in a storm at sea—not a severe one that howled and raged, tossing the ship about like a doll.

Devin touched her arm, his gentleness a balm to her soul.

"Trinity, you do not have to marry me. If you oppose our union, I shall figure out something else to keep you safe in Casablanca."

"Unless we are married, there isn't a way. Morocco is not England. Our ways are not theirs."

Once she had put aside her feelings and examined the situation with logic and pragmatism, Trinity knew what to do. Keep her emotions under careful control, do not fall in love with the handsome rogue, and make the best of an awful situation.

"Even then, according to Mrs. Peagilly, I might not be. She'd hired guards to protect us, and now that she is gone…"

A shiver zipped across her shoulders.

Devin gave one stern nod. "The captain said as much too."

Her stomach pitched to her toes at that affirmation.

She *had* made the right choice.

Somehow, she would make this union work.

"Just so you know, men hired to protect me, and now you, Trinity, are meeting the ship. I have also retained Mr. Amzil to act as our eyes and ears in Casablanca."

"I like him." Trinity did.

She plucked her cloak off the peg beside the door. Legs braced, she draped its woolen length over her shoulders.

"I delayed long enough to write a contract with the terms we discussed." Devin patted his chest, causing the paper to crackle. "It is brief, as there was not time to write a detailed legal document. I made a copy for you too."

"Thank you." Her estimation of Devin rose again.

Amid this gale and likely feeling unwell, he'd had the forethought and consideration to honor his word. Even if he had not followed through with the promise, Trinity would've accepted his protection but only as his wife. She was a survivor.

Ideals, principles, and ethics did little to provide security, safety, and protection. Devin could do all three.

"Any luck?" He glanced past her to the table where the satchel still reposed.

He needn't specify what he meant.

"No." Trinity shook her head. "I do not think Mrs. Peagilly was accustomed to sharing her plans. Perchance because she had been alone for so long. I did find her itinerary. We were to have gone to Greece next. I have never been." She shrugged. "In any event. There is nothing among her effects that helps me. Us."

This was not just about her.

Outside, the storm shrieked her rage, and a shiver of fear assailed Trinity for the first time.

"Only her will, a solicitor's name, a contact in Casablanca, a bank receipt, and a few other items."

Making a sound in his throat, Devin swiped a sopping strand off his forehead.

After securing the clasp, she glanced up. "Is the captain in his cabin then?"

"No." He shook his head. "The storm came upon us unexpectedly and is severe. He cannot spare a minute more."

"I have never been aboard a ship during a storm."

Trinity tried to sound brave, but being at the ocean's mercy proved unnerving, even for someone who'd sailed as much as she had.

For Devin, it must be worse.

Strain emphasized the contours of his face, which held a distinct greenish tint.

"Captain Breckett said to send for him when we were ready." Concern leached into his voice. "The contract can be witnessed at the same time."

"Very well." Trinity staggered, and Devin steadied

her. "Given the strength of this storm, we'd best hurry before the captain cannot leave the bridge."

After blowing out the lamp, Trinity stepped into the passageway, and once she'd secured the cabin door, they made their way toward the captain's quarters in silence.

Despite her outward composure, she was on the verge of either hysterical tears or frenetic laughter—perchance both.

Mr. Amzil, as saturated as Devin, lingered near the bottom of the gangway.

Ah, the messenger.

"Please let the captain know we shall await him outside his cabin," Devin said.

Mr. Amzil's kind gaze shifted between Trinity and Devin before he broke into a toothy grin.

"Yes, sahib. Right away, sahib." He climbed three treads before turning halfway and calling, "Congratulations."

Devin took Trinity's arm to steady her as they stumbled toward Captain Breckett's quarters.

Even her stomach rebelled at the churning motion.

She slid Devin a sideways glance.

A muscle ticked in his jaw, a testament to his rigid self-control. As long as he did not cast up his accounts during the ceremony. What a retelling that would make.

That thought took her aback.

Lord, the entire situation was like a bad gothic novel.

In truth, she would rather not explain why she and Devin married.

I was stranded in Morocco, possibly at risk of being abducted and sold into slavery.

Devin wanted his mother to stop meddling and trying to arrange a marriage for him.

Two perfectly wonderful reasons for agreeing to spend the rest of your life with someone you scarcely know, yes?

Trinity clenched her teeth and hands against a nervous giggle.

When she'd joined the captain in his quarters earlier today, she could not have imagined that she would be returning in a few hours to exchange wedding vows with Devin.

"I am afraid Sir Godfrey has retired for the night, so our only witnesses shall be Mr. Alderton and the captain."

"I suppose that is fine."

What did she know of such things?

"May I ask your full name and how old you are, Trinity?"

Trinity stared at him for a heartbeat.

Good Lord, he was marrying her without knowing such basic details.

"Trinity Samantha Honoria Shepard Ablethorne. All the girls from Haven House and Academy were given Shepard—an altered version of Shepherd—as their name in honor of the childless proprietress, Mrs. Hester Shepherd, just as all of us received a silver cross when we left the academy."

"The one you were wearing earlier today?" He gestured toward the area where she had pinned the cross this morning for Mrs. Peagilly's service.

"Yes." She nodded. "Oh, I shall be six and twenty in December."

Outside the captain's quarters, Devin pulled Trinity into his arms and pressed a swift kiss to her trembling lips.

"I am sorry this is rushed and not more romantic."

Despite the tremor his kiss sent through her and the surge of desire heating her blood, she curled her toes in her boots and remained aloof.

"It is not as if we are wedding for love, Devin. Our union is based on desperation on my part and convenience on yours. Let's not pretend it is anything else."

To prevent further loss of life and the spread of the dreaded disease, we urge you to close the ports and cities' gates as you have ordered during previous plagues. At the very least, quarantine Tangiers, where the plague originated.

~Several Foreign Consuls,
in an entreaty to Sultan Moulay Suleiman

Captain Breckett's Cabin
Five minutes later

*D*evil take it.
  I shall not vomit. I shall not vomit.

Standing before Captain Breckett, rain dripping from his oilcloth into puddles on the floor, Devin steeled his resolve. He would be cursed, by Hades, if he would heave his hash while citing his marriage vows.

A sideways glance at Trinity revealed her waxen pallor as well.

If the situation was not so deuced horrible, it might be funny.

The storm had not abated a jot but, rather, seemed to have grown in ferocity.

"Let us get on with it." Rubbing his chapped hands together, Captain Breckett did not even consult *The Book of Common Prayer*. "I am needed topside, and both of you look like you should find the nearest berth and lie down."

It was true.

Trinity had grown wanner by the minute, and if Devin did not lie down soon, no force on earth or heaven could keep the contents of his stomach in place. Even then, he was not positive he'd not spend his wedding night heaving until his throat burned.

"If you have no objections, I shall skip the more poetic verses." Grizzled eyebrows high on his broad forehead, the captain looked between Devin and Trinity. "Agreed?"

Devin nodded, and Trinity whispered, "Yes."

Gripping her elbow to steady her, Devin gave her a reassuring squeeze.

Her weak smile was anything but encouraging.

In less than three minutes, they recited their vows, the captain entered the marriage in his logbook, and he and Mr. Alderton witnessed the contract Devin had scribbled for Trinity amid the ship doing her utmost to toss him on his arse.

"Congratulations, Mr. and Mrs. Everingham." Captain Breckett shook Devin's hand. "I shall record the marriage when I return to England. There will be no doubt you are legally married." Cheeks apple red, he scratched his bewhiskered jaw. "As long as...ah...the marriage is consummated."

Tight-lipped, Trinity nodded.

Had she been concerned about that?

Fiend seize it.

Devin ought to have considered her unease. He had no intention of consummating their vows on a ship bucking like a wild horse.

The ship shuddered as wind and sea pummeled her with the vengeance of a prizefighter.

Casting an experienced glance ceilingward, the captain said, "I suggest you remain in your cabin until the storm passes." He shifted his gaze to Mr. Alderton. "With me, Mr. Alderton."

"Aye, aye, Capt'n." His nose a red beacon, Mr. Alderton made a half bow. "Felicitations. May ye be happy."

Hat clasped in his weathered hands, he shuffled his feet and cast the captain an apologetic glance. "It doesna seem proper no' to offer ye a blessin'."

Mìle fàilte dhuit le d'bhréid,
Fad do ré gun robh thu slàn.
Móran làithean dhuit is sìth,
Le d'mhaitheas is le d'nì bhi fàs.

150

A thousand welcomes to ye with yer marriage.
May ye be healthy all yer days.
May ye be blessed with long life and peace,
May ye grow old with goodness, and with riches.

"Thank you, Mr. Alderton. That was lovely." Trinity graced him with one of her breathtaking smiles, and the little man flushed red to his ears.

"Indeed," Devin managed, only sounding half-strangled.

The blessing was the only thing even halfway romantic about the wedding. When they returned to England, if Trinity wanted to, they'd have a proper ceremony.

Wearing a surprisingly tolerant expression, Captain Breckett waited just outside the doorway.

Mashing his hat upon his head, Mr. Alderton bobbed a farewell.

Leaving the door open in their wake, he and the captain rushed down the passageway. Their haste could probably be attributed as much to the howling wind as having left Compton in charge during the ceremony.

Oh, to have been a fly on the wall when Captain Breckett explained that he was turning the bridge over to the second officer to perform Devin and Trinity's nuptials.

"Shall we?" Devin extended his arm, and she placed her fingertips on his sleeve.

His bride had wilted considerably these past few minutes.

This storm tested even the strongest stomach.

Sliding an arm around her waist, Devin guided her from the captain's quarters to hers.

Once inside, her cloak still on and the door ajar, she sagged onto the lower bunk, limp as wet straw, and raised soulful blue eyes to his.

Did he dare light her lamp?

A sudden lurch almost sent him headfirst into the berth.

Probably wise not to take a chance.

"Some wedding night, huh?" she muttered. "Both of us sick as dogs."

The shadowy interior hid her delicate features, but her tone conveyed her weariness and wariness.

Bollocks.

They ought to have discussed the delicate subject before exchanging vows.

Not sure how much longer he could remain standing, Devin waved his hand toward the bunk. "May I?"

"Of course." Nodding, the movement indistinct in the muted light, she scooted over. "If I am this miserable, I imagine you are worse."

Devin would rather not dwell on that truth and hoped the chamber pot was within reach beneath the bunk. His desire to comfort Trinity outweighed his need to keep from humiliating himself in front of her again.

After shutting the door, he sank beside her and took her cold hand. "I think we should wait to consummate our vows."

She made a little sound in her throat.

"Firstly, this is not the ideal setting." He gave the bunk a sardonic glance, though she could not see it. "Secondly, because circumstances rushed our union, we should spend time getting to know each other. This trip can be our honeymoon. 'Tis a little backward, but we are both up to the challenge."

"Yes. I think that is wise too." Tangible relief tinged her tone.

Devin drew her into his arms as he reclined against the pillows. The bunk was not too crowded if they both lay on their sides.

Settling against him, she sighed.

"Will we laugh about this someday, Devin?"

"I honestly do not know."

"It is the nonsensical stuff of which romance novels are made, is it not?"

Was it?

"Just rest, sweeting." Devin closed his eyes, praying for sleep to overtake him before sickness did. Pressing his lips to her forehead, he breathed in her sweet scent. "Tomorrow, we arrive in Morocco, and our adventure as husband and wife begins."

14

*You dare to presume to tell me, the almighty sultan,
how to govern my land? I remind you, each time the
plague reached this sacred country, it was because of
foreigners bringing the disease to our shores. My people
cannot suffer another long season of quarantining and
closed borders. It is in Allah's hand who lives and dies.
I leave it to His will.*

~**Sultan** Moulay Suleiman, in response to
the impudent petition from the foreign consuls

*Trinity's cabin
Early the next morning
24 October*

Having been emersed in the loveliest dream, Trinity
tried to shove her growing alertness away. She did
not want to wake up. Even between restless bouts of
fitful sleep, niggling away at the back of her
consciousness was the knowledge that she'd married
Devin.

She married a man she scarcely knew because when
the *Daunting Duchess* reached Morocco, she would
have been on her own if it weren't for Devin.

As she slowly let slumber slip away, she became

aware of a firm body entwined with hers. Her head lay on Devin's broad shoulder, one arm flung across his torso.

One of his arms held her to him, and his other hand cradled her hip.

Their entwined legs made it impossible to rise.

In truth, it was a rather pleasant way to awaken.

Opening her eyes, Trinity edged her chin upward to trace her gaze over his features. Dark stubble shadowed his jaw and chin, and those thick lashes she envied lay like lush fans atop well-defined cheeks.

Mouth parted, he snored gently, his chest rising and falling in a steady rhythm.

They both must've fallen asleep quickly.

A blessing that had saved her from humiliating herself by being sick in front of him.

The ship no longer rose and fell in undulating waves, nor did the dual sounds of the ocean beating against the hull as wind ravaged the vessel carry into the cabin.

What time was it?

"Good morning, wife."

Devin gave her hip a slight caress, his voice a husky rasp.

Rather than take offense or call him to task for his forwardness, Trinity reveled in his touch and the tingling that radiated outward from where his hand cupped her hip.

She'd never denied her attraction to Devin, even if it had not been wise. Now that they were married…

"Good morning."

Pushing herself onto her forearms, Trinity gazed down at him. In the low light, his face softened by sleep, his hair tousled, and his mouth curved into a drowsy half-smile, he appeared almost boyish. "I think the storm is over. How do you feel?"

Eyes slightly narrowed, he considered the question before a naughty grin twisted his mouth. "Very nice, thank you."

Good heavens.

She practically lay prone atop him, chest to chest, thigh to thigh, only her gown and his pantaloons between them.

"Yes, well…" She tried to leverage upward, but her skirts and his legs entrapped her. "A little help, please."

He gripped her ribs, probably to lift her off him.

Instead, she dissolved into giggles.

"Are *you* ticklish?" Delight tempered Devin's voice as he wiggled his fingers along her ribs, sending her into another fit of laughter.

"Yes." Twisting and writhing, she slapped at his hands.

"Stop. Devin. Please stop."

"Hmm, I require a forfeit."

"Forfeit?" she asked breathlessly.

"Indeed. A kiss should suffice." He formed his mouth into an exaggerated pucker.

"For shame, Devin. You are nothing but an opportunist."

Laughing, Trinity shoved at his chest. "You would use extortion?"

He gave her a wicked grin.

"It is not every day I wake up with my luscious wife draped across me. We did not have a wedding night. I think a good morning kiss is a fair exchange."

"Very well." She dropped a brief kiss on his mouth, but he did not release her. Instead, he splayed his hands wide over her shoulder blades.

"You will have to do better than that, my love." Devin's voice dropped an octave, causing a delicious tremor to vibrate through Trinity.

If he wanted a toe-curling kiss, by thunder, she would give him a toe-curling kiss.

Trinity grazed her lips across his once. Twice.

His breathing quickened, but he did not become the aggressor.

A sense of empowerment made her bold. Lowering her head, she traced her tongue over the seam of his mouth.

Tensing beneath her, Devin dug his fingers into her sides.

Oh, this was interesting. Most interesting indeed.

Trinity licked his lower lip, grinning when a guttural growl reverberated in his chest.

Enjoying the tantalizing exploration, she settled her mouth upon his, replicating the sensual movements he had taught her last night.

Had it truly only been last night that they'd first kissed?

Devin threaded a hand into her hair at the back of her head, holding her in place as the kiss grew more intense and arousing.

Trinity was not certain when she lost the advantage and Devin took control. Not that she minded. Her bones had turned to pudding, every nerve sensitized and attuned to the man beneath her as her head swam in a fuzzy, heady haze.

So this was desire.

Time ceased.

Only this moment mattered.

This joining of souls.

Trinity had no idea how long they kissed, and she quite forgot why she'd kissed Devin, to begin with. Only this time with him mattered. This moment. This memory in the making.

Finally, he gently pulled his mouth away.

Her forehead resting against his and lost in wonder and foreign feelings, Trinity willed her breathing and pulse to regulate.

"Will that suffice?"

Good heavens.

Did that throaty voice belong to her?

"That more than sufficed, sweeting. Much more of that, and I promise, our marriage would've been consummated."

"Oh."

That was unexpected.

Still, she could not prevent a tiny spark of feminine pride.

In a deft movement, Devin maneuvered her off of him, then rose from the bunk. One arm braced on the upper berth, he gazed down at her.

"I need to freshen up. Breakfast with me afterward?"

His abrupt withdrawal momentarily stunned her. Somewhat mollified at his invitation, she brushed the hair off her face and nodded.

"I would like that."

How could she refuse?

This man was her husband, and Trinity wanted to make this unconventional marriage work.

His answering grin would've enchanted the goddess Venus herself from the cloud she reclined upon. And Trinity, a mere mortal, could not resist his charisma. He had slowly been bewitching her since she helped him that first night aboard the ship.

Devin straightened, then stretched his arms wide. His muscles must be stiff from the cramped quarters and Trinity's weight upon him for God only knew how long. Mayhap all night. "I shall return in half an hour. Does that give you enough time for your ablutions?"

"Yes." She swung her legs over the edge of the bunk, exposing most of her calves.

A mischievous smile playing around the edges of his mouth, Devin retreated a step, allowing her to stand.

"Trinity?"

She gazed up at him, this man who was now her spouse. How easy it would be to love him. But could she trust him? Odd that love came easier than trust.

"I shall be a good husband to you." He drew a finger along her jaw, his expression tender and sincere. "I vow it."

How Trinity wanted to believe him—wanted to believe this forced marriage of convenience could turn into something more. What had started as a solution to a mutual problem might become an answer to prayer— a blessing even. But that was the stuff and nonsense of which fairytales were made, not real life.

"And I shall try to be a good wife."

And she would.

How horrible the many years stretching before her might be if she grew bitter and shrewish. In truth, she was not certain what constituted a good wife, having no example to follow.

Surely, it could not be all that challenging.

Should she tell Devin now that cooking wasn't her greatest skill?

Perhaps not just yet.

She did not want to ruin this enchanted thing between them.

"Then, I would say, Mrs. Everingham, that we are off to a grand start."

A knock on her door caused them to swing their heads toward the panel. Though they were married, heat swept her from waist to hairline. This marriage business would take some getting accustomed to.

"Yes?" she called.

"Captain had a wedding breakfast prepared for you and Mr. Everingham, lady," came Mr. Amzil's familiar voice. "It awaits you in the saloon."

"Thank you." She met Devin's gaze. Did everybody know they'd married last night? "Everyone is going to think..."

She could not say it aloud. Likely everyone aboard the ship except Gladys and Georgie thought they knew what had happened in this tiny cabin last night.

Devin cupped her chin, grazing his thumb over the small indentation.

"We know the truth. That is all that matters." Devin's expression grew grave.

"We must always be honest with each other, Trinity. Must always communicate what is in our hearts and make every effort to understand, support, and respect the other, even when we are angry or disappointed. I promise I shall. Can you do the same?"

Such earnestness riddled his tone and emphasized the contours of his face that she could not deny him. Nor could she make such a sweeping promise because the truth of it was that she did not know if she could. So she settled on the truth, which was what he had asked for first.

"I shall try, Devin. I truly shall."

15

I regret to inform you that your mother passed. I arranged to have her buried next to your father. My sincerest condolences. Two servants also died, and I advanced funds for their burials. The London house remains closed with only a skeletal staff. I have sent this message to the Chouara Tannery. Hopefully, it will find you there or at your next scheduled stop.

~Mr. Milton Shillingford, in a short note
to Devin Everingham
sent on the *Mystique* to Morocco but not delivered,
as Devin had already sailed back to England

Port of Casablanca
Three days later—mid-morning

Devin glanced at his wife, standing beside him and taking in the bustling port as the crew and laborers positioned the gangway. She sent him a beatific smile, excitement dancing in her eyes as she took in the unfamiliar landscape.

The beastly storm had blown the ship off course, resulting in their delayed arrival.

Not that he'd minded. The extra days aboard the vessel had allowed him to get to know Trinity without the demands, responsibilities, or concerns he could expect once they disembarked. For those few days, she had his complete attention and devotion.

Several other ships lay anchored in the harbor away from the pier—a row of enormous wooden ducks. Likely, the *Daunting Duchess* would also move to deeper water after unloading her cargo.

Once the workers secured the plank, Captain Breckett and his officers stood nearby to welcome two official-looking gentlemen aboard, white kerchiefs obstructing their lower faces. Several more men lingered near the bottom of the gangway, many with cloths drawn over their noses and mouths as well.

Compton had not spoken a word to Devin since his marriage to Trinity.

The man pouted worse than a petulant wallflower during her first *haut ton* season.

Devin scanned the active pier, taking in the many cultures, diverse clothing, and the cacophony of languages, animals, and a multitude of carts and wagons.

It was a wondrous, chaotic scene.

Drawing his eyebrows together, he brushed his hand over his chin.

Was it typical for so many people to have their faces covered?

His contact, Mrs. Peagilly's, and the entourage for the McKinnicks were probably among the individuals the captain had yet to welcome onto his ship.

Yes, there to the side, away from the others, stood eight smartly uniformed soldiers attired in British red and white. Something other than sweltering heat had them shifting restlessly and darting wary gazes here and there.

The four McKinnicks, Meriwether, and Truman-Shelton had assembled farther along the ship's rail. Curiously, neither Meriwether nor Truman-Shelton had pursued the conversation about a business venture with Devin. Mayhap they'd rightly concluded he was not easily swindled.

Neither had he warned Compton to be wary of the two. Compton was a grown man, capable of making his own decisions.

"Isn't it something, Devin?"

Trinity stood on her toes, craning her neck as she leaned over the rail.

He wrapped an arm around her waist lest she fall.

"Careful, darling. You do not want to tumble overboard."

The endearment, one of many he had uttered in recent days, fell from his lips as naturally as breathing air. Without effort or even awareness on Trinity's part, his wife had burrowed her way under his skin and into his heart. The vixen had not asked permission but had taken up residence there, and now Devin could not conceive a future without Trinity.

Was this love?

This consuming desire to be with her?

She dominated his thoughts when they were apart, and he found himself daydreaming of their future together. Of the dark-haired children they would have. After they had their fill of traveling the world, that was.

Unlike his father, Devin wanted his wife at his side on his sojourns.

He was not so jaded that he did not believe in love. In truth, a few of his friends swore the sentiment had transformed the former rakes and rogues into ideal husbands. Devin just never expected to fall so quickly and so hard.

It simultaneously terrified him and left him giddy as a lad.

Look what had happened to Father.

Yes, but Trinity was not like Devin's mother in any fashion. She did not care about rank and status. About *le beau monde* and blue blood. About wealth and power and prestige.

Thank God.

Today, she wore her pretty pink gown again.

However, instead of the heavy spencer, she had draped a light shawl about her shoulders and wore a wide-brimmed straw bonnet to protect her face from the unrelenting sun.

She was a breath of fresh air in the stifling heat, and she was his.

Devin had not told her he was falling in love with her.

He was not quite ready to make that confession.

Instead, he savored the knowledge and pondered the wonder of it in his heart. Primal instinct told him she wasn't ready to hear his declaration yet. He needed to build her trust first.

Trust and love: a solid foundation for a marriage and a future.

Then when he became confident that she felt the same way, they'd consummate the marriage. Celibacy wasn't new to him, though he had not been a monk. Waiting until Trinity was ready was another method of gaining her trust.

He would wait as long as necessary.

No one suspected they had not completed the act yet. Devin endured the sly winks and crude jokes from the male passengers and crew in his stride. He'd also explained to Trinity that they'd need to share a cabin at night for the rest of the voyage to secure the illusion of intimacy.

An intelligent woman, she had understood the necessity and agreed without a fuss.

At night, when they lay together, arms round one another, and spoke of their pasts and hopes and dreams for a future—those were the hours Devin most cherished and looked forward to.

One of the official-looking men, a tall, thin chap with a wizened face above his kerchief, stopped six feet from Captain Breckett and extended a packet, forcing the captain to stretch his arm to accept the neat bundle.

Most peculiar.

The other gentleman, skin as smooth and dark as molasses, did the same with Mr. Compton, handing him a short stack of letters tied together with a string.

No doubt correspondence for those aboard the ship—crew and passengers alike.

That officer made a smart bow before turning on his booted heels and retreating with great alacrity. The gangway jostled with each precise step he took in his hasty return to the dock.

Compton untied the string and flipped through the top few letters.

A frown skewered his brow before he glanced up and glared at Devin, then shifted his peeved gaze toward Trinity, still enthralled with the port activity.

Presenting his back to the curious onlookers aboard

the ship, the other man spoke to Captain Breckett and Mr. Alderton in subdued tones.

Mr. Compton stomped across the deck, his boots clumping loudly with each angry step. He shoved two letters toward Devin.

"These are for you, Everingham."

He extended another toward Trinity.

"This one is addressed to Mrs. Peagilly. You might find it helpful." At her hesitation, his features softened. "There is no harm in opening it now."

"Thank you." She turned the neatly folded rectangle over but did not crack the coffee-brown wax seal.

Without another word, Compton marched toward the McKinnicks.

Devin expected his correspondence to pertain to his reasons for coming to Morocco. Indeed, the first was from Jalil Dhabi, the overseer of the Chouara Tannery. However, rather than news of the leathery, the contents were short and disturbing.

Plague.

Sweet Jesus.

God help them.

God help the Moroccan people.

They'd just endured the plague, and to have it upon the population again...

Devin kept his countenance neutral, despite the alarm tunneling through his veins.

This changed everything.

Was that why so many people had their faces covered?

Was it more than a local custom?

Were some of these people here because they sought a way out of Morocco?

There was no question of him visiting the leatherworks now.

He veered Captain Breckett a sideways glance, taking in the captain's black expression and Mr. Alderton's taut features.

Yes, they'd just learned the drastic news too.

Devin dropped his gaze to the second letter and scowled.

From Shillingford.

How had it made it to Morocco before Devin had?

Ah, the storm had delayed the *Daunting Duchess*, but that meant Shillingford had posted the letter right after Devin left London.

Had mother refused to go to Essex?

It was just like her to stir up a fuss.

Had God ever made a more obstinate woman?

Well, at least he'd thwarted her plans to select a bride for him. She would be livid, particularly that he had married a commoner.

Mother would never have considered Trinity good enough, but she was exactly what Devin needed and wanted. She made him happy, and that was priceless.

He did not need to remain away from England for years anymore, although he still intended to look in on his various enterprises around the world. Only now, it would also be his honeymoon.

Or it would've been had he not just learned that plague infested the area. There would be no visiting the leatherworks or exploring the country.

"Is all well, Devin? You look upset."

Trinity laid her hand on his arm, her pale blue eyes searching his before she shifted her attention to the letter he gripped in his fisted hand. Even though he had tried to hide his troubled musings, she'd sensed them.

They'd been like that from the beginning—attuned to each other in a way that mere words could not define.

He forced a reassuring smile.

"An unexpected letter from my man of affairs. My mother is probably giving him fits. I love her, but she is quite insufferable."

"I am sorry." She nestled into his side, fitting there as if molded to do so.

He'd told Trinity all about his mother and father. She was the only person he had confided such intimate details to. She'd been surprisingly compassionate toward Mother, explaining that constant disappointment may have turned her bitter, and she had eventually targeted Devin's father with her animosity even though it had not been his fault.

What Devin had done to deserve Trinity, he would never know.

With another wry smile, he used his thumb to break the wax. He went rigid after reading the first paragraph, then, with his heart battering his ribs, skimmed the rest in a rush. His breath left his lungs in a harsh exhalation.

"Devin?"

"My mother. She is very ill." He raised his gaze to Trinity's—hers round pools of concern and sympathy. "The physician says I should return to England immediately."

How?

The *Daunting Duchess* had no passenger accommodations available.

What about the other ships?

He scanned the harbor.

At least ten ships lay anchored there.

Conceivably, they were also fully booked with passengers hoping to escape the plague. Would the ships' captains allow possibly infected travelers on board, risking they might spread the disease to other ports?

No wonder the officials boarding the *Daunting Duchess* had used such precautions.

"Oh, Devin. Of course, we must." Wrapping her arms around his waist, Trinity hugged him, uncaring that public displays of affection were not *de rigueur*.

"It may be too late already." He stared blindly over her head. "She made me bloody angry, and I despised her interference, but…"

Devin could not finish the sentence.

He swallowed the emotion throttling up his throat.

To not be able to say goodbye—to see his mother one last time.

The notion was unbearable.

"What does Mrs. Peagilly's letter say?" Devin could guess.

Trinity slid a finger beneath the wax on the letter for Mrs. Peagilly.

He folded his notes and slid them into his coat pocket, his mind racing.

They must find passage home.

It did not matter how much it cost or how uncomfortable the accommodations might be.

All the color drained from Trinity's face, leaving her waxen and shaken.

"Lord, no," she whispered.

Just as Devin had suspected.

"Devin?" She held the slip of paper between trembling fingers. "There is plague here. Mrs. Peagilly was told not to come. Her interpreter has died, and what is more, the hotel we were to stay at was damaged in a fire."

Devin cradled Trinity in his arms. "My other letter was from the tannery overseer. He said the same, love."

Mrs. McKinnick let out a small shriek and clutched her children to her skirts. So, the McKinnicks had learned the awful truth as well.

"I do not care if you lose your position, Godfrey," she wailed. "I shall not risk our children's lives. I am not, I repeat, *not*, setting foot ashore."

Clutching Gladys's and Georgie's hands, she practically dragged her children to the hatch.

Meriwether and Truman-Shelton exchanged horrified glances before charging toward the captain, jabbering like old tabbies.

What was the protocol in a situation like this?

Devin was a partial owner of this ship, yet he did not have a blasted idea.

"What are we to do?" Trinity asked.

"I am going to speak with the captain." Devin owned this ship—well, part of it. By thunder, that counted for something. "I do not care if I have to sleep on the deck, this ship is returning to England, and we are going to be on her."

16

There was nothing to be done. I could not, in good conscience, force any crew members or passengers to disembark the ship in Morocco, nor could I risk taking infected persons aboard. It weighs heavily upon me as captain of this vessel and a man of God.

I pray for the souls I left behind and ask that God forgive me if I made the wrong decision. I intended to save as many lives as possible by reducing the plague's spread.

At Mr. Everingham's directive as a partial owner of the ship, and with my full cooperation and agreement, I have given the order to weigh anchor and return to England, our cargo intact.

~Captain Horatio Breckett,
in the *Daunting Duchess's* logbook

London Harbor
Four and a half days later—early evening
1 November

Trinity clutched Devin's arm as they disembarked the ship. Back in London's damp and chill, less than a fortnight after sailing away that fateful night full of hope and expectations. Fate must be having a good laugh.

Blessedly, the weather had cooperated the entire voyage, even providing a welcome tailwind to speed them along the route home. Other than a minor bout of nausea, Devin had not suffered from seasickness on the return voyage.

Hopefully, that meant his constitution was similar to hers, and he would not become sick on future voyages they enjoyed together.

Other than Mr. Amzil, whose fear for his family outweighed any concern for his personal safety, no one else had set foot in Casablanca. Mr. McKinnick had not needed much persuasion by his adamant—nearly hysterical—spouse to forsake his diplomatic appointment. Given the circumstances, he felt confident the British government would understand and assign him a different post. If not, he vowed that he had no regrets about sacrificing his career to ensure his family's wellbeing.

Even Misters Meriwether and Truman-Shelton had confided over supper last night that they had decided to put aside their entrepreneurial business enterprises in favor of less perilous ventures in England. Trinity still wasn't convinced either man could be trusted, but at least they had not swindled anyone aboard the *Daunting Duchess*.

Thank goodness the voyage was relatively brief, as

far as voyages go, and there had been no shortage of staples or food.

Devin revealed that Captain Breckett refused to permit a single barrel, bundle, pallet, or crate to be loaded onto the ship from the port of Casablanca. Nonetheless, it had taken all afternoon to persuade East Indie Dock authorities not to quarantine the ship's crew and passengers.

"I shall have a devil of a time convincing the investors and merchants that returning to London without delivering or picking up cargo was the best financial decision," Devin said. "But you cannot put a price on lives. Had they been in my place, I would hope they'd err on the side of caution too."

Two laughing urchins ran by, their clothing ragged and patched but their faces clean. An equally shabby dog, his tongue lolling and adoration in his gaze, trotted beside them. Trinity had always wanted a dog, but traveling as she had these many years did not allow her the opportunity, and none of her previous employers had pets.

She swept Devin a contemplative glance from beneath her lashes. He said he would like a dog. Mayhap they could get a puppy.

The voyage home had been four of the happiest days of her life, and by the time the *Daunting Duchess* anchored, Trinity had no doubt she had fallen completely, irreversibly, and happily in love with her husband. They'd yet to consummate their marriage, but she felt certain they would do so soon.

She quite anticipated becoming Devin's wife in every way.

With him, Trinity could envision a future she'd never before let herself imagine. Dreams she had long ago shoved to fusty corners to molder, she could now drag out, dust off, and permit to become a reality.

It wasn't just that he was considerate and tender, kind and fair, but he was also funny, had a mischievous streak, and made her feel like the most beautiful, desirable woman who'd ever walked the earth.

Oh, she still harbored misgivings and uncertainties about Devin. Not the solicitous, considerate man aboard the ship, but the rakehell she'd witnessed at the Mumfords' house party.

Which was the real Devin?

Perhaps both aspects were.

Complex and multifaceted, did people change as their circumstances altered, or was behavior a result of human will or inherent instinct?

She glanced over her shoulder at the sailors behind her and Devin carrying their luggage on muscled shoulders. He had arranged to have their trunks delivered to his London house.

Captain Breckett had ensured Trinity that Mrs. Peagilly's nephew would collect her belongings.

Accustomed to traveling light, Trinity owned little in the way of material possessions, so when Devin said he would like to purchase her an entirely new wardrobe, she had not known how to respond. Of course, now that she was married to one of London's wealthiest men, she must present herself appropriately for her new station.

Only, she still wasn't entirely certain what that was. Neither did she want to parade about in the first tulip of fashion and draw undue attention to herself.

A glossy black carriage pulled by a pair of stunning ebony horses drew to a halt before them. A coachman in a smart black wool greatcoat climbed down.

"That is my coach," Devin whispered in her ear, his breath tickling the sensitive flesh and causing a delicious shiver to flutter up her spine. "Though I do not know how they learned we had arrived."

A tidy gentleman attired in the first stare of fashion and sporting a rather magnificent mustache stepped from the carriage.

"Ah, Shillingford, of course." Humor, admiration, and respect colored Devin's words. "I vow, the man has eyes and ears everywhere. I do not know what I would do without him."

"Welcome home, sir." Shillingford's curious gaze shifted to Trinity.

"Thank you, Shillingford." Devin drew Trinity forward. "Allow me to present my wife. Trinity Everingham. Trinity, this is Milton Shillingford, my man of business."

Other than an eyebrow creeping upward a quarter inch, Mr. Shillingford's demeanor changed not a jot. Commendable control, that.

The drivers, on the other hand, exchanged flabbergasted glances.

Mr. Shillingford bent into a respectful bow.

"I am *delighted* to make your acquaintance, Mrs. Everingham."

Trinity did not miss the emphasis he placed on delighted. Nor the approval shining in the man's eyes.

"And I yours." She dimpled at him, and he produced a smile so broad his eyes nearly disappeared into his cheeks.

Jaw slack, eyes moonlike, Devin gawked.

"Shillingford, in all the years I have known you, never have you more than twitched your mouth upward a quarter inch. And yet you are grinning like a buffoon at my bride. What has this world come to?"

"You have not given me a reason to smile before, sir," his man of affairs replied drolly.

Shillingford was happy about Devin's unforeseen marriage?

Well, that was a good start.

"My coachmen, Jim Jones." Devin gestured to the seated driver, then the chap holding the coach door. "And Tim Jones."

"Twins?" Trinity narrowed her eyes, glancing between them before she threw up her hands. "I vow, I cannot tell you apart."

"Oh, you will learn soon enough, Mrs. Everingham. I am the more handsome twin," Jim said with a friendly wink.

Or was he Tim?

"I am the more charming and intelligent," his twin quipped.

"You will be searching for new positions if you continue this fribble." Shillingford's stern visage did not seem to affect either of the men.

Trinity laughed. "I shall have to pin colored ribbons on you to start, or else I shall never know which is which."

"We used to trade places to fool our mum," said the still-seated twin.

"Aye, and had our ears boxed aplenty for our pranks," the other replied.

Shillingford signaled to a pair of dock workers,

who promptly began loading Devin's and her luggage into a nearby wagon.

"Shall we?" Mr. Shillingford extended his arm, and Devin assisted Trinity into the plush coach. Dove gray velvet covered the bench and squabs. "I am afraid there is only a skeletal staff at the house—the housekeeper and footman. Tomorrow, I shall see to recalling the servants that were sent away to prevent infection. You'll also need to hire two housemaids."

Devin settled beside her and took her hand in his.

How naturally Trinity and Devin had fallen into the roles of husband and wife.

Mr. Shillingford's eyes twinkled in approval.

Tension radiated from Devin, and he shifted restlessly.

He had fretted about his mother between bouts of guilt for leaving England without bidding her farewell. Having never had parents, Trinity could not truly understand the complexities of parent-child relationships.

Despite Devin's frustration and irritation with his mother, Trinity knew he loved her. He'd said so many times as he shared childhood stories.

"My mother?" He met Shillingford's unwavering gaze.

Devin's man of business slid his focus to Trinity,

sending her a silent message before returning his attention to his employer.

Instantly, she knew. Somehow, she *knew*, and her heart broke for Devin.

Clasping his hand firmer, she pressed into his side, willing him to absorb her strength and comfort.

"I am sorry, Devin." Mr. Shillingford gave a sad shake of his silvery head. "I sent a letter, but the ships must've crossed."

"She...she died?"

Such agony contorted Devin's features and distorted his voice that Trinity bit the inside of her cheek.

"She *died*?" he repeated, shaking his head in denial. "I came straight back. We did not even disembark. We had a strong tailwind. It only took four days."

Did he speak to them or himself?

Trinity wept inside but refused to let her pity show. Devin would hate it.

He snapped his head up. "When?"

"The day I sent the first letter." Shillingford crossed his legs. "I had her buried beside your father at Seybrook Manor in Essex."

Closing his eyes, Devin rested his head against the squabs. "Fitting since that is where I intended to banish her for the remainder of her life."

"Devin, you could not have known."

Trinity tried to soothe him, but consumed with guilt and self-loathing, he could not hear her.

"If I had not been so determined to spite her. To make her stop meddling and interfering." His harsh, scornful laughter filled the coach as Mr. Shillingford looked on with understanding and compassion.

Pain blazing in his eyes, Devin speared Trinity a scornful glance. "You are everything my mother would've despised in a wife for me. Precisely why I picked you."

Choking on a gasp, Trinity recoiled.

Mr. Shillingford made a rough sound in his throat, but Trinity could not bear to look at him. To see his pity or his embarrassment on her behalf.

Devin's hurting, she reminded herself.

Do not take anything he says at this moment to heart.

How could she not?

Gone was the considerate, charming man aboard the ship. She did not know this cold, harsh, caustic person. Perhaps he wasn't as different from his mother as Devin would like to believe.

Trinity bit her tongue to keep from blurting those unkind words.

Mrs. Shepherd's admonition, "Out of the

abundance of the heart, the mouth speaks," sprang to mind. How often had Mrs. Shepherd warned her charges to guard their hearts and words?

Toward that end, Trinity pressed her lips together and set her jaw. She would not make matters worse by responding in kind—even if Devin deserved a verbal lashing.

God rot the...the...*rotter.*

A stilted, strained silence descended upon the coach, growing ever more palatable and tense as the horses *clip-clopped, clip-clopped* their way toward Berkeley Square. Finally—thank God, for Trinity wanted to scream and tear at her hair—the vehicle slowed, then stopped before a stately stone mansion.

Not ostentatious, but decidedly upper crust.

One of the twins, Trinity had no idea which, opened the door and helped her descend.

She half-turned, waiting for Devin to join her.

Not the happy homecoming she had hoped and prayed for them.

Mr. Shillingford climbed out next, and after offering Trinity a heartening smile, he also faced the carriage. "Sir?"

Devin spoke from the darkened interior, his tone cold, flat, and emotionless.

"Help Trinity inside, Shillingford. See that she has

everything she needs. I am going to Essex. I do not know when I shall be back."

Humiliated to her core, Trinity could not say a word. Only stood mute, shaking from cold, mortification, and powerful rage that almost choked her as she watched the coach carrying her new husband away until it disappeared.

Devin had abandoned her.

Dumped her on the stoop and left without a backward glance.

She refused to let the tears flow. Hands fisted, she swallowed and blinked the moisture away.

Shillingford's pitying glance nearly undid her, but she notched her chin higher.

You're everything my mother would've despised in a wife for me. Precisely why I picked you.

Each clipped word, the monologue playing over and over in her head, stabbed Trinity, creating oozing wounds. Wounds that would take a long time to heal.

"He did not mean it, Mrs. Everingham," Mr. Shillingford said kindly as he guided her up the steps.

She shot him a cynical glance. "I think we both know he did."

"He would not have married you for that reason alone," he said. "Of that, I am positive."

Bless the man for trying to make her feel better.

Devin still had no excuse to treat her like a soiled news sheet. The sting of anger heating her blood, she glanced down the street. Well then, she would give her husband of fewer than two weeks a reason to treat her like rubbish.

"Mr. Shillingford, may I presume when my husband said that I am to have everything I need, that includes funds? A carriage? A horse? A lady's maid? New furniture? A puppy? Pineapples? Turkish Delight? Sugar plums?"

What other ridiculous luxuries?

"Indeed, madam. I believe those are *all* necessities." He rapped upon the indigo door.

"A talking parrot?" She gave him a wicked grin. "No, a *swearing* parrot."

Devin said he wanted a parrot. Trinity would find the most foul-mouthed fowl ever to hatch.

The man of business burst into laughter. "An absolute essential."

"Ah, then I should like to go shopping on the morrow, Mr. Shillingford."

"An excellent notion." The door opened, and Mr. Shillingford escorted her inside. "My wife always finds a shopping excursion most revitalizing and a boon to her constitution."

Trinity permitted another naughty grin. "Oh, trust

me, Mr. Shillingford. My constitution shall be *completely* invigorated by the time I am done."

Then she would seek an annulment. For, by all that was holy, she refused to spend the rest of her life with a man who could so easily discard her.

Revenge might be a little bit sweet, after all.

17

I have just returned to London, and I am married. Can you come for tea this Thursday? I shall explain all then. It is quite a tale, I assure you. I also need your advice, discretion, and influence.

I need an annulment as quickly as possible.

~ Trinity Everingham in letters to her girlhood friends: Joy Morrisette, Mercy Brockman, Chasity Terramier, Purity Rutland, and Faith Kellinggrave

Devin's Berkeley Square house stables
Fifteen days later
A quarter of ten in the evening

B one weary from having ridden straight from Essex, only stopping long enough to change horses, Devin left the exhausted gelding in the stables. Mile after mile, he had chastised himself with blistering castigations for being an utter arse.

He would not be surprised to find his bride had left him, though where Trinity would go, he did not know. She had a few friends in England, but he had not bothered to find out who they were.

That truth only reaffirmed what a selfish blighter he was.

If she had gone, he would turn London—no, all of England and beyond—on its head to find her. She was the best thing to ever happen to him, and he'd ruined it. Somehow, he had to make it right. Even if it took months. Years. A lifetime.

He must tell her he loved her.

Even if she threw the words back in his face.

Devin had deserted Trinity—his beautiful, sweet bride—on their first night back in London. He had left her with a skeletal staff she did not know and to manage a strange house when she had no experience with such matters. But far worse, he'd made her a target for gossip amid a society not known for its kindness and acceptance.

Knowing Shillingford would ensure she did not want for essentials did nothing to ease his mind. She did not care about possessions and things. Trinity had told him that.

It had taken a week of berating himself for fleeing his mother and mourning her passing to come to his senses. Leaving his bride, the woman who'd captured his heart and shown him nothing but kindness, compassion, and gentleness, was a far worse offense than escaping a woman hell-bent on finding him a bride of her choice.

Fate or providence or perhaps God Almighty had

brought Devin Trinity. A far better wife than he could've imagined and certainly beyond anything he deserved.

His cruel words haunted him—bludgeoned him.

Lord, how they must've eviscerated Trinity.

You're everything my mother would've despised in a bride for me.

God above, that utterance had been inexcusable, was deserving of purgatory, but the rest—

That is precisely why I picked you.

Recalling Trinity's stricken expression gutted Devin. She had done nothing to deserve his cruelty. Like a wounded animal, he'd lashed out when she only tried to comfort him.

Another week of drowning his sorrows—a first for him—and trying unsuccessfully to blot the memory of that night from his mind had passed.

Two things brought him to his senses.

The first was an unsettling dream, so real that he expected to see his parents in a lush garden when he awoke. His mother and father—holding hands, laughing, and appearing happier than he could ever remember them being—strolled a magnificent garden path.

They paused, staring at him with such intensity that his nape hair raised even now.

"You have made a terrible mistake, Devin," Father said. "One you'll regret the rest of your life."

"Hurry back to her, son." Mother smiled up at Father, their love surreal. "Before it is too late."

The second, a terse letter from Shillingford, launched Devin from his chair and onto a horse within half an hour.

To Hades with coaches. They took too long.

~*~

> *Mrs. Everingham seeks an annulment and uses powerful friends to accelerate the process. I would advise you to return to London post haste.*
>
> *I have also included a letter from your mother that she dictated for you when she knew she would not recover. Had you not left that night, I would've given it to you then.*
>
> *By the by, your wife has spent nearly five hundred pounds, with my blessing. She is intent on acquiring a swearing parrot.*
>
> *M. Shillingford*

~*~

The letter from Devin's mother proved the healing balm

his heart craved. She had not been angry with him, nor did she blame him. If Mother could forgive him, then he needed to forgive himself and return to Trinity. And pray that she could forgive him.

He could make things right between them. He must.

Devin slipped in the side door, using a key hidden beneath an innocent-looking rock. He'd used that method of exiting and entering the house since before his university days when his parents had one of their roof-raising rows.

He slipped off his boots, left them beside the door, and ascended the first stairway.

On silent feet, he padded through the house, the polished parquet floor not revealing his presence. Flames flickered in the wall sconces as he made his way toward the second staircase.

He paused, searching the corridor, seeking a telling glow beneath the library, study, or drawing room doors.

Nothing.

Trinity must be upstairs.

Please let her be upstairs.

His wife, his love.

A few minutes later, he stood outside the only room with light seeping beneath the door.

Should he freshen up first?

He had bathed last night and donned fresh clothing

this morning. Still…

"Come here, my darling." Trinity's voice filtered through the door.

What the devil?

"It is time for bed, sweetheart, and I sleep much better with you snuggled beside me."

No. No.

He was too late.

Chin tucked to his chest, Devin braced a hand against the doorframe, struggling to drag breath in and out of his lungs. A clock struck the hour somewhere in the house, its rhythmic chiming a stab of pain with each peal.

Devin had come home to declare his love and adoration, but Trinity had invited another into her bed.

Before they'd even consummated their vows?

How the devil did she hope to attain an annulment if she was not chaste?

If he had not left…

Devin did not care if he smelled like a horse's back end. No blackguard was climbing into his wife's bed, making Devin a cuckold.

"Trinity!" he bellowed as he flung the door open to the bedchamber his mother had always referred to as the garden chamber.

Hand-painted silk wallpaper bedecked with pastel

flowers, vines, and birds adorned the walls. Floral brocades in pinks and yellows covered the armchairs, hung from the windows, and covered the cushions and counterpane. Potted ferns on white wicker stands stood before the windows as a fire crackled merrily in the tiled hearth behind a scrolled screen.

A single candle on the classical Italian inlaid nightstand illuminated the feminine room.

He pointed his livid gaze at the bed with its gold-carved headboard.

No hairy, muscled man—naked or otherwise—lay sprawled there.

Shrieking, Trinity yanked the bedclothes to her chin, her blue eyes wide and frightened.

She should be alarmed.

Devin's heart cracked further with every agonizing beat.

Too late. Too late. Too late.

She'd found another.

"Where is he?"

Devin stomped into the room, looking this way and that, scraping every corner and shadow with his furious inspection.

"I know he is in here. I heard you talking to him."

"Who?" She eyed him warily, her forehead puzzled in genuine confusion.

He shoved the draperies aside.

No man lurked there.

He charged to the wardrobe and yanked the doors open.

Only gowns—lots and *lots* of new, expensive, high-fashion gowns—met his furious scrutiny. To be certain no bounder hid behind the silks and satins, he shoved an arm between several.

"Have you lost your mind? Barging into my chamber without so much as a by-your-leave." Ire flashed in Trinity's eyes as she lowered the sheet a few inches.

She had plaited her sable hair, the long braid draped over one shoulder, and she wore a chaste white nightgown buttoned to her chin.

Not the most romantic of nightwear, though she'd never looked more beautiful to him.

Hands on his hips, Devin searched the room with his gaze again. "I know the blighter is in here."

He did not have time to escape through the window into the garden below.

Aha. The blackguard hid under the bed.

He strode forward, and Trinity shrank back against the pillows.

"What are you doing?" She held out an unsteady hand. "Stay there, Devin."

"It did not take you long to find someone to warm your bed," he snapped. Furious with himself. Furious with Trinity. Bloody furious with the libertine hiding in this room.

"Still, I blame myself. I should've been here. Should've treated you with dignity and respect."

She canted her head, but her gaze remained flint-like. "Yes, you should have done."

"I heard you tell him it was time for bed. That you sleep better with him beside you." Stooping, he tried to see beneath the bed. Not an easy task with the bed skirt obstructing his view.

"*What*?" Her voice pitched high.

He speared her a don't-you-dare-deny-it scowl.

"You think...?" Trinity giggled, those gorgeous blue eyes sparkling with mirth. "You believe...?"

She dissolved into another fit of giggles.

"I am heartily gratified that *you* think it is funny," Devin all but growled.

How could he be simultaneously incensed and wounded to his soul?

Heartbreak was a very real thing, indeed.

"Oh, it is funny. Hilarious, in truth, and when you realize what an...an..." Forehead furrowed and lips pursed, Trinity appeared to search for an appropriate insult before her face lit up. "What an absolute *assling* you have been, you will grovel at my feet."

"I think not." Determined to find the bounder, Devin kneeled, placing one hand on the bed for balance.

A moment later, needles pierced his fingers.

"What the blazes?" He jerked his hand away and met the black eyes of a petite bundle of gray fur.

Grrr. The poodle puppy crouched, his wiggling bottom in the air. *Grrr.*

"He wants to play with you," Trinity said softly.

Devin closed his eyes.

Lord, have mercy.

He had made a horrible situation worse.

Much, *much* worse.

And yes, he would be groveling.

Cracking an eye open, he took in the pudgy pup.

"*He* is who you were talking to?"

"I am not an adulterer, Devin."

Proud and defiant, Trinity lifted her chin.

"Even if *that* is precisely the kind of woman your mother would've despised and precisely why you chose me."

"Oh, God." He sank onto his heels. "I have made an utter arse of myself again. Worse, I have hurt you, sweetheart. Again. Of course, you are not an adulterer. You are everything pure and decent. Remarkable and marvelous."

She gathered the puppy into her arms, where he settled contentedly, his curious little button-eyed gaze riveted on Devin.

He stroked the puppy's curly back. "What is his name?"

Instead of answering, Trinity asked coldly, "Why are you here? Why now? It has been over a fortnight. I have already begun looking into an annulment."

"I know. Shillingford wrote to me."

She snorted, hurt and betrayal marring her precious visage. "You did not want me, but you come trotting home the instant you think I do not want you? Is that it?"

"No. I came to apologize." Devin touched her hand. "To beg your forgiveness. I was wrong, darling. So wrong. I know that now. I had to face some ugly truths about myself, and at the end of everything, only one thing mattered. You."

Trinity's eyes filled with tears before she averted her face and buried it in the puppy's soft fur. "Fine, you have apologized. I forgive you. Now, please leave."

"No, my heart. I cannot." Devin pressed her hand to his cheeks, unashamed of the moisture also trailing from his eyes.

"I love you, Trinity. I shall do whatever it takes to make you believe me. To give us a future together."

18

I vow you the first cut of my meat,
the first sip of my wine,
from this day it shall only be your name
I cry out in the night
and into your eyes that I smile each morning;
I shall be a shield for your back as you are for mine.
Nor shall a grievous word be spoken about us,
for our marriage is sacred between us,
and no stranger shall hear my grievance.
Above and beyond this,
I shall cherish and honor you through this life
and into the next.

~Traditional Celtic Wedding Vow

Still in Trinity's chamber

I shan't cry in front of him. I shan't.
Why did Devin have to say he loved her?

And Lord, help her. Fool. Fool. *Fool*. Trinity believed him.

Men did not fake emotion the way some women did. That this strong, confident man had been brought to tears by declaring his love for her eviscerated Trinity.

She could've resisted anything else. Her heart resonated with answering love, and the three little words were right there—on the tip of her tongue, eager to spring forth. Regardless, she could not say them.

He had shattered her trust.

In him. In herself. In them.

She set Stormy aside, tucking the puppy beneath the coverings.

"You just accused me of adultery, Devin."

Her words sounded hollow even to her ears.

"I was a stupid, jealous fool, and I give you my word that it shan't happen again." Devin kissed her fingertips. "I have made a mess of things, but I want to make it right. Nothing is as important now, or will ever be, as you are. Tell me what I must do to make it right."

"I do not know, Devin."

Trinity closed her eyes.

She was so tired.

Tired of weeping. Tired of glancing at the window, hoping to see him—dreading that she might. Tired of listening, always listening, for him to come home. And then, when he did, the first thing he did was accuse her of adultery.

"On the ship, everything seemed so right between us." Slowly, she lifted her lashes. "I did not expect a fairytale. I knew we'd have difficult times because we'd married hastily. I was prepared to deal with that. To try, really try to make our marriage work."

"We *can* make it work," he vowed.

Devin seemed so earnest—so sincere.

How she wanted to believe him—needed to believe him.

"I shall never disrespect or disregard you again. You are too precious to me. I love you so much that it makes me stupid with giddiness. I want the whole world to know." He touched her cheek. "And I think... I hope that you love me too."

Trinity dropped her focus to the sheets across her lap. Running her fingertip across the crocheted edge, she firmed her lips.

If she said the words, she was lost.

No. She was strong. Resilient.

Love was wonderful. Marvelous. Exhilarating. Healing.

She had to choose to trust Devin, to let their love live, thrive, and grow, or she'd crush the gift out of self-preservation and fear of being hurt.

"Trinity?"

Slowly, afraid that he would see the truth in her eyes, she forced herself to meet his smoldering brown gaze.

"How can I make you believe me, my darling? How can we start over?"

She searched his face, seeking the answer they both needed.

"I do not want to start over," she whispered.

His face fell, pain and regret sharpening his features.

"I want to build on what we had…what we have." She managed a tremulous smile. "I do forgive you." She laced her fingers through his, nearly undone because her heart was so full of love. "And I do love you."

He was beside her on the large bed in an instant, gathering her into his powerful embrace. "Thank you. Thank you. Thank you."

Stormy popped his little head up and, with a whimper, crawled on top of them and licked Devin's face.

"He likes you." Trinity patted Stormy's head. "I named him Stormy because of the storm the night we married."

Devin grinned and gave her a swift kiss.

"Well, the little chap needs to find a different place to sleep tonight, for I intend to show my lovely bride just how much I love her."

Trinity cocked an eyebrow. "Oh, you do, do you?"

"I do," Devin growled into her neck, nipping the tender flesh there.

"He has a basket in the corner over there." She pointed to an area beside the armoire.

Devin rose and scooped the little fellow into his

arms. After he'd settled Stormy in his bed, he strode to the door. "I shall be back in five minutes."

After he left, Trinity jumped from the bed and raced to the bureau. She flung garments right and left until she found the night rail she had bought on impulse. Even after he had left her, a part of her still hoped they could be man and wife. A filmy Egyptian-blue, lacy confection, it assuredly was not meant for warmth or modesty.

She swiftly unbuttoned her nightgown, pulled it off, and slid the silk nightgown over her head. It settled in a soft woosh around her ankles.

Unplaiting her hair, she dashed to her dressing table and ran the brush through the thick strands. On impulse, she dabbed perfume behind her ears, at her wrists, and then, with a naughty smile, between her breasts.

She'd just blown out the candle and hopped into bed when Devin gave a brief knock and slipped into the room.

Lord, he was gorgeous, sleek, sinewy masculinity.

Hair damp, he only wore a black and gold striped velvet banyan.

Appreciation for her change of gowns glowed in his eyes.

Instead of getting into bed, he sat on the edge, grazing his fingers across her cheek.

"Are you sure, Trinity? We can wait."

"I am sure, Devin."

She reached for him, brushing her fingers through the dark hair on his chest. The crisp hairs tickled and aroused. "I only needed to know you loved me."

He slid out of his robe and between the sheets. "Until the stars fall from the sky and the oceans dry up. I shall never stop loving you."

He caressed her hip.

"Nor I you. I am ready to be your wife in every way."

She sighed as he ran his fingers down her back, then over her buttocks.

"Will you marry me, Trinity?"

She tilted her head. "We are married."

"No. Let's have a real ceremony. A traditional wedding with your friends. Mine. Shillingford. Whoever you want."

"I would love that, but right now, I would rather concentrate on other more tantalizing and intriguing things."

"Tantalizing and intriguing, you say?" His voice dropped to a throaty rasp as he trailed a finger across her collarbone.

"Oh, yes."

Epilogue

On my employer's behalf, I wish to reserve furnished houses with servants on Santorini overlooking the Aegean Sea for the month of May and in Athens for the month of June.

He is interested in purchasing an estate in Greece as well.

Please send descriptions, locations, and pricing of properties that meet the criteria I have included on the last page of this letter.

~Mr. Milton Shillingford,
in a letter to his business contact in Greece,
Bakchos Demotropolis

Berkeley Square-London
20 November 1820
The wee morning hours

For the umpteenth time, Devin glanced at the white onyx mantel clock.

Nine minutes past three.

It would not be long now.

But the blasted doctor and midwife had been saying that for the past two hours as Trinity labored to bring their first child into this world. Whoever said women were the weaker sex had obviously never been present when a babe was born.

Though Doctor Travers harrumphed his disapproval and Mrs. Todd regarded Devin as if he had leprosy, he had refused to leave Trinity. Why should he get to sleep when agony ripped her asunder?

Eyes squeezed shut, she groaned and gripped his hand so tight that his fingertips grew numb.

"Push, Mrs. Everingham. Push." At the end of the bed, Mrs. Todd glanced over Trinity's bent knees and offered an encouraging smile. "You're wee one is almost here. Push."

With a guttural, animalistic cry, Trinity clenched her teeth and pushed.

A second later, the most tremendous, joyous sound Devin had ever heard filled the chamber.

His child's cry.

He had a child.

A babe he would raise to know unconditional love and acceptance.

"My baby," Trinity whispered, lifting her head as she tried to see the infant Mrs. Todd cooed to as she wiped the birthing blood off the child.

Devin wiped a damp cloth over Trinity's sweat-slickened brow.

Doctor Travers made a note in his journal,

recording the babe's time of birth.

"Congratulations, Mr. and Mrs. Everingham. You have a daughter."

Eyes wide with wonder, Trinity met Devin's eyes. "We have a daughter."

He kissed her, loving her impossibly more at this moment than he could comprehend. "You were marvelous, darling."

Mrs. Todd placed the wrinkled, red-faced, squalling wonder in Trinity's arms.

"Look at all that hair," the midwife said.

"She is beautiful," Trinity whispered.

Devin wisely did not suggest otherwise.

"Hello, my precious." Hearing her mother's voice, the babe stopped crying and gripped Trinity's finger. Their daughter opened her eyes. Blue.

Of course, they would be blue.

The doctor and midwife tended to the afterbirth before tidying the chamber.

Devin kissed his daughter's forehead and then stared in awe.

He and Trinity had created this tiny, helpless being.

Tears welled in his eyes.

Patting the bed, Trinity scooted over, unable to hide a wince as she did so.

"Devin, lie beside me."

Ignoring the doctor's scowl, Devin did as his wife bid. He wrapped an arm around her back so her head rested on his shoulder. They stared at their baby for several blissful moments as she peered up at them.

"I shall call upon you tomorrow, Mrs. Everingham." The doctor and Mrs. Todd slipped from the bedchamber, leaving the new family alone.

"Aurora Bryony Hope Everingham," Trinity murmured sleepily. "I hope you have many brothers and sisters."

Since neither he nor Trinity had siblings, they wanted a large family, God willing.

She glanced up at Devin. "I love you."

"I love you too, my heart." He kissed the crown of her head.

True to his word, he had spent every day since the night he'd returned to London being the best husband he could be. He had even taken to reading the Bible as Trinity faithfully did. In that, too, he'd found peace and comfort he'd never known.

As his beloved wife and their daughter drifted to sleep, Devin closed his eyes and sent a silent prayer heavenward.

Thank you, Lord.

About the Author

USA Today Bestselling, award-winning author COLLETTE CAMERON® writes Scottish and Regency historical romance novels featuring dashing rogues, rakes, scoundrels, and the strong heroines who reform them. Blessed with an overactive and witty muse that won't stop whispering new romantic romps in her ear, she's lived in Oregon her entire life, although she dreams of living in Scotland part-time. A confessed chocoholic and dachshund lover, you'll always find a dash of inspiration and a pinch of humor in her sweet-to-spicy timeless romances®.

Explore Collette's worlds at collettecameron.com!

Join her VIP Reader Club and FREE newsletter.
Giggles guaranteed!

FREE BOOKS: Join Collette's **The Regency Rose®
VIP Reader Club** to get updates on book releases,
cover reveals, contests, and giveaways she reserves
exclusively for email and newsletter followers. Also,
any deals, sales, or special promotions are offered to
club members first.

http://bit.ly/TheRegencyRoseGift

Follow Collette on **BookBub**
www.bookbub.com/authors/collette-cameron

From the Desk of Collette Cameron

Thank you for reading LADY TEMPTS A ROGUE, the final book in my DAUGHTERS OF DESIRE (SCANDALOUS LADIES) series. While this story is a sweet Regency romance with inspirational overtones, I also attempted to introduce romantic elements tastefully.

I conducted a tremendous amount of research for this story. As always, I strive for as much historical accuracy as possible while still providing a romantic novel.

The instrument that Devin played in the story is known as an Ocarina. These vessel flutes date back to the medieval era, are found in many cultures, and are made from clay, porcelain, and wood. The night telescope was invented in 1810, and when Trinity looked through Mr. Compton's, it was still a relatively unrefined tool.

I took artistic liberty regarding English diplomats and military existence in Morocco in 1818. The presence of consuls from other countries is well-documented, even during The Tangier Plague, though I could not find specific mention of the British.

The plague did indeed reach the port of Tangiers in 1818 and lasted in Morocco through 1820. Although Sultan Moulay Suleiman was asked to quarantine the Port of Tangiers because the plague was present on vessels in the harbor, he refused. His sons were aboard one infested vessel. In this case, unlike previous plagues, the government did little to prevent the spread of disease caused by Oriental rat fleas carrying the bacterium Yersinia Pestis.

A myth long accepted as factual is that sea captains could perform marriage ceremonies while at sea. In the United States and Britain, it was expressly forbidden to do so unless the captain was also a pastor, justice of the peace, or a judge. I could not find specific regulations on what waters qualifying captains could perform marriages, so I added the restriction of only doing so in international waters.

The Chouara Tannery still exists in Fez, in the Souq leather bazaar. This tannery is the oldest in Morocco and still uses the same methods to create extremely soft leather that readily absorbs the dye as it has for a thousand years.

I have another important point I would like to mention briefly. Readers outside the United States have become upset that I use American spellings in my Regency and Scottish stories.

Multiple factors influence an author's decision about which spellings to use for their books. I chose American spelling simply because most of my reading audience is American, and my books are published in America. While I stick to a few British rules, such as *I shall* and *I shan't*, instead of *I will* and *I won't*, I have not extensively adopted other British grammatical rules and spelling. I believe my readers are flexible enough to adapt to slightly different spellings.

After all, it is the romance novel that matters, right?

To stay abreast of the releases of my other books, please subscribe to my newsletter (the link is below) or visit my author world at collettecameron.com.

If you enjoyed Trinity and Devin's story, please consider leaving a review on BookBub, Goodreads, or individual book vendors. Reviews truly do help authors and are so appreciated.

Hugs,

Collette

Connect with Collette!
Join her Facebook Reader Group:
    www.facebook.com/groups/CollettesCheris
BookBub: bookbub.com/authors/collette-cameron
Facebook: facebook.com/collettecameronauthor
Instagram: instagram.com/collettecameronauthor
Goodreads: goodreads.com/author/Collette_Cameron
YouTube: youtube/ColletteCameronAuthor

Made in United States
North Haven, CT
06 March 2023

33681491R00122